new edition

THE LIFE AND ADVENTURES of SANTA CLAUS

WRITTEN BY
JULIE LANE

ILLUSTRATED BY
HOKIE

first edition by SANTA CLAUS PUBLISHING CO.

NEW EDITION   PARKHURST BROOK PUBLISHERS

This edition is dedicated especially to Steve, who would have laughed with us about another vast project - and also to the kids, without whom the idea might never have happened: Cary, Jack, Lindsay, Jeff, Kady, Heidi, Elisabeth, Julia, Joey, Jake, Justin, Laura, Colby, L. J., Joey III, Meggy and Danny.

Copyright, 1932
By Santa Claus Publishing Co.

This edition, copyright 1985
by Parkhurst Brook Publishers
Potsdam New York

Second printing 1986
Third printing 1990
Fourth/Fifth printings 1993
Sixth printing 1994

Library of Congress
Catalog Card Number:
85-61987

ISBN 0—9615664—18
Manufactured in the U.S.A.

CONTENTS

new edition SUPPLEMENTAL TEXT BY THE CHARLEBOIS FAMILY 145–154

SUPPLEMENTAL ILLUSTRATIONS BY JIM BAXTER

The old head drooped drowsily.

DRAW close to the fire, all you who believe in the spirit of Christmas, whether you call it Santa Claus, or simply good will to men; and listen to the story of Nicholas the Wandering Orphan who became Nicholas the Wood-carver, a lover of little children. Follow him through his first years as a lonely little boy, who had the knack of carving playthings for children; then as a young man, busy over the little toys; then as a prosperous, fat, rosy old man, who overcomes all sorts of difficulties in order to attain his ambition, a toy for every child in the village. Learn how he started to drive a beautiful sleigh drawn by prancing reindeer; why he first came down a chimney; how he filled the first stocking; where the first Christmas tree was decorated; and finally how he came to be known as "Saint Nicholas" and "Santa Claus."

this book belongs to

To order additional copies of this book, see page 153.

"He's a good lad."

CHAPTER 1
NICHOLAS LOSES HIS FAMILY

NCE upon a time, hundreds and hundreds of years ago, in a little village on the shores of the Baltic Sea, there lived a poor fisherman and his wife and their two children — a four-year-old son, Nicholas, and a tiny baby girl, Katje. They were only poor fisherfolk, and their home was a simple, one-room cottage, built of heavy stone blocks to keep out the freezing north wind, but it was a cheery little place in spite of the poverty of its occupants, because all the hearts there were loving and happy.

On cold winter nights, after the fisherman had come home from his hard day's work out on the open sea, the little family would gather around the broad open fireplace, — the father stretching his tired limbs before the warm fire, puffing peacefully at his after-supper pipe, the mother knitting busily and casting now and then a watchful eye on the two children playing on the floor. Nicholas was busy over a tiny piece of wood, which he had decked with gay bits of cloth and worsted, while little Katje watched him with round, excited blue eyes, finally reaching out her eager, fat little hands to take the doll Brother Nicholas had made for her. The glad crowing of the baby over her new toy aroused the father, who turned to look at the scene with amused eyes, and then a rather disapproving shake of the head.

"Eh, Mother," he said, "I'd rather see Nicholas down at the boats with me learning to mend a net than fussing with little girls' toys and forever carrying Katje about with him. 'Tisn't natural for a boy to be so. Now when I . . ."

"Hush, man," interrupted the woman. "Nicholas is hardly more than a baby himself, and it's a blessing that he takes such care of Katje. I feel perfectly safe about her when she's playing with her brother; he's so gentle and sweet to her. Time enough for him to be a fisherman when he grows too old to play with his baby sister."

"True enough, wife. He's a good lad, and he'll be a better man for learning to be kind to little ones."

So for another year Nicholas went on fashioning rude

little playthings for Katje, and the mother went about her many household tasks busily and happily, and the father continued earning his family's daily bread in the teeth of biting gales and wild seas. In this way the little family might have gone on for years, until the father and mother had grown old, until Katje had become a beautiful young maiden taking the burden of the housework from her mother's shoulders, and until Nicholas had become a tall, strong youth, going out every day in his father's little fishing boat. All this might have been, but for the events of one wild, tragic night.

Little Katje lay in her crib tossing feverishly. The mother bent over her fearfully, taking her eyes from the hot little face only to glance anxiously now and then towards the door, and straining her ears between each wail of the sick baby for sounds of footsteps on the stone walk outside the cottage. For the father was late, — late to-night of all nights, when he was needed to run to the other end of the town for the doctor. As the minutes dragged on, the storm outside grew in fury, and the fear in the woman's heart over the absence of her husband and the painful whimpering of the child finally goaded her into action. She arose from her position beside the crib

{ 3 }

and swiftly putting her shawl over her shoulders, spoke to Nicholas, who was trying to comfort little Katje.

"Listen, my son," she said quickly, "your father is late and I'll have to go for the doctor myself. I'll have to leave you alone with Katje. You'll take care of her, won't you, Nicholas, until Mother gets back? Just see that she stays covered, and wet this cloth now and then for her poor, hot little forehead."

Nicholas nodded solemnly — of course he would take care of Katje. The mother patted his head and smiled, and then was out in the wet, black, windy night. And Nicholas watched Katje until she suddenly stopped tossing the coverings aside, and her hot little forehead grew cooler and cooler and then cold to his touch; and as the embers in the fireplace grew black and then gray, his head nodded, and he fell asleep on the floor beside the crib.

And that's the way the villagers found him the next morning, when they carried home his father, drowned when his boat was caught in the storm, and his mother, stricken down by a falling tree. So, of the once happy little family of four, there was now only Nicholas, the orphan.

CHAPTER 2
HIS FIRST CHRISTMAS GIFT

HE fishermen of the village smoked one pipe after another, and scratched their heads for a long time over the problem; their good wives gathered together and clacked their tongues as busily as their knitting needles; and the main topic of every conversation was — "What is to become of that boy Nicholas?"

"Of course," said fat Kristin, wife of Hans, the rope-maker, "no one wants to see the child go hungry or leave him out in the cold; but with five little ones of our own, I don't see how we can take him in."

"Yes," chimed in Mistress Elena Grozik, "and with the long winter well set in, and the men barely able to go out in the boats, no fisherman's family knows for certain where the next piece of bread is coming from. And with the scarcity of fuel . . ."

All the ladies shivered and drew closer to Greta Bavran's comfortable log fire, and sighed heavily over their knitting.

Mistress Greta arose and poked the fire thoughtfully.

"We could take him for awhile," she meditated aloud. "Jan had many a good catch last season, and we have somewhat laid by for the winter. We have only the three children, and there's that cot in the storehouse where he could sleep . . . Mind you," she interrupted herself sharply as she noticed the look of relief spreading over the others' faces, "mind you, we might not have a crust to eat ourselves next winter, and besides, I think everybody in the village should have a share in this."

"Quite right, Mistress Bavran," spoke up another. Then, turning to the group, "Why can't we all agree that each one of us here will take Nicholas into her home for, say a year, then let him change to another family, and so on until he reaches an age when he can fend for himself?"

"I suppose Olaf and I can manage for one winter," said one woman thoughtfully.

"You may count on me," added another. "Not for a few years, though; we have too many babies in the house now. I'll wait until Nicholas gets a bit older."

Greta Bavran gave the last speaker a sharp look. "Yes, when he's able to do more work," she muttered under her breath. Then aloud — "There are ten of us here now. If we each agree to take Nicholas for a year, that will take care of him until he's fifteen, and without a doubt, he'll run away to sea long before that."

The ladies laughed approvingly, then feeling very virtuous at having provided for Nicholas until he reached the age of fifteen, they arose, wrapped up their knitting, and proceeded to wrap themselves up in shawls and woolens before going out into the sharp winter air.

"Will you find my Jan at the shop, and tell him to fetch Nicholas from the Widow Lufvitch where he's been staying?" called Greta after the last woman.

"That I will, Greta; then I must hurry to my baking. I almost forgot the Christmas feast tomorrow, with all this talk about the orphan."

So it was that Nicholas came to his first home-for-a-year on Christmas Eve, to kindly people who tried their best to make a lonely little five-year-old boy forget the tragic events of the past week. In spite of the festivities of the day, he curled himself up in a corner of the storeroom, and with heartbroken sobs for his lost mother and

{ 7 }

father and beloved Katje, tried to drown out the sounds of merrymaking in the cottage. But the door opened, and a little form was seen in the ray of light.

"What do you want?" asked Nicholas almost roughly. "Go away; I want to be alone."

The other little boy's mouth quivered. "My boat's broken," he cried, "my new boat I got for the Christmas feast, and Father's gone out, and Mother can't fix it." He held up a toy fishing boat.

Nicholas dried his eyes on his sleeves and took the broken toy in his hands. "I'll fix it for you," and he turned back to his corner.

"Oh, come in here where there's more light," said the youngest Bavran.

So Nicholas went in where there was more light, and more children, and more laughter.

As the year passed, the little boy gradually forgot his grief in the busy, happy life of the Bavran household. The other three children played with him, quarreled with him, and came to accept him as one of themselves. Nicholas, in his turn, was not too young to appreciate the happy year he spent with his new brother and sisters, and when he heard talk in the household that Christmas Day would

"What do you want?" asked Nicholas.

soon bring to a close his stay with the Bavrans, his mind was confused with many different thoughts. There was sorrow in his heart at leaving, a fear of what unknown life was awaiting him in the next house, and a growing desire to do something, no matter how small, to show his benefactors how much he loved them and their children. The only things he owned in the world were the clothes he wore, an extra coat and trousers, a sea-chest and a jack-knife which had belonged to his father. He couldn't part with any of these, and yet he wanted to leave some little gift. A happy thought struck him — Katje had always loved the little dolls and animals he had made for her out of bits of wood; maybe now, with the help of the jack-knife, he could fashion something even better. So, for the last two weeks of his stay, he worked secretly in the dark storeroom, hiding his knife and wood when he heard anybody approaching, and struggling furiously the last few days so that all would be finished by Christmas morning; because, since it was Christmas when the Bavrans had taken him last winter, he must be passed along in exactly a year's time.

The toys finally were finished. Nicholas gave them a last loving polish, and looked at them admiringly — a handsome doll, dressed in a bright red skirt, for Margret, the eldest; a little doll-chair, with three straight legs and one not so straight, for the next little girl, Gretchen; and a beautiful sleigh for his playmate, Otto.

So the next day, when the three children were weeping loudly as they watched the little sea-chest being packed, and their father was waiting at the door to take Nicholas to Hans the rope-maker's house, the departing orphan slowly drew from behind his back the rough little toys he had made, and forgot to cry himself as he watched the glee with which the children welcomed their gifts. And a lovely glow seemed to spread itself over his heart when he heard their thanks and saw their happy faces.

"Well, I'll be going now. Good-by, Margret; good-by, Gretchen; good-by, Otto. Next year I can make the toys better. I'll make you some next Christmas, too."

And with this promise, Nicholas bravely turned his back on the happy scene, to face another year some place else. His small form looked smaller still as he trudged along in the snow beside the tall figure of Jan Bavran. His thin brown face, surrounded by a shock of yellow hair, seemed older than his six years, saddened as it was by this parting, but the blue eyes were still gay and warm at the thought of the happiness he had left behind him.

"Well," he thought to himself as they approached the rope-maker's house, "maybe the five children here will be just as nice to me as the Bavrans, and I can make toys for them, too. Christmas can be a happy day for me, too, even if it is my moving day."

 **To talk about the special meaning of this chapter**

turn to page 145

{ 12 }

HE Christmas days that followed were happy, not only for Nicholas, but for all the children he met in his travels from house to house. At the rope-maker's cottage, most of the winter evenings were spent by the children learning to wind and untangle masses of twine, and to do most of the simple net-mending. Nicholas discovered that by loosening strands of flaxen-colored hemp he could make the most realistic hair for the little wooden dolls he still found time to carve. When he left at the end of the year on Christmas Day, the rope-maker's five little children found five little toys waiting for them on the mantel of their fireplace, and Nicholas did not forget his promise to the three Bavrans, but made a special trip to their house Christmas morning with their gifts.

And so it happened, as the years went on, and Nicholas

{ 13 }

grew more and more skillful with his father's jack-knife, that the children of each household came to expect one of Nicholas' toys on Christmas Day. Not one child was ever disappointed, for the young wood-carver had a faculty for remembering exactly what each child liked. Fishermen's sons received toy boats built just as carefully as the larger boats their fathers owned; little girls were delighted with dolls that had "real hair," and with little chairs and tables where they could have real tea-parties.

All this time, Nicholas had been busy with many other things besides toy-making. As he grew into a tall, strong boy, there were many tasks in which he had his share, and which he did willingly and well. In the spring, he learned to dig and plant the hard northern soil with the vegetables the family lived on during the winter; all summer he helped with the boats, mended nets, took care of chickens, cows, horses, and in one well-to-do household, even reindeer. He was an especial favorite with the mothers, because the babies and younger children would flock to Nicholas, who would play with them and care for them, thus giving the tired mothers a chance to attend to the housework. During the winter months, Nicholas attended school with the other boys and girls of the village, learning his

{ 14 }

A B C's in exchange for carrying in the wood for the schoolmaster's fire.

So on one particular winter's day we find Nicholas on his way to school, trudging along a snowy country road, dragging behind him a sled loaded with logs of wood. He is now fourteen years old, a tall, thin boy, dressed in the long, heavy tunic coat of the village, home-knit woolen leggings, and a close-fitting black cap pulled down over his yellow hair. His eyes are blue and twinkling, and his cheeks rosy from the keen winter air. He whistles happily, because, although in a week it will be Christmas-time once more, and he will have to make his final change, he remembers the chest full of finished toys — one for every child in the village. It is the first year he has been able to do this, and the thought of his trips on Christmas morning, when he will personally deliver to every child one of his famous toys, makes him almost skip along, burdened though he is with the heavy sled of wood.

Finally he reached the yard of the schoolmaster's cottage, and was immediately attracted by the group of schoolboys, who, instead of running about playing their usual games and romping in the snow, were gathered together in one big group, excitedly discussing something. As

Nicholas entered the yard, they rushed over to him and began talking all at once, their faces aglow with the wonderful news they had to tell.

"Oh, Nicholas, there's going to be a race . . ."

". . . on sleds — Christmas morning — and the Squire is going . . ."

". . . He's going to give a prize to the one who . . ."

"No, let me tell him. Nicholas, listen. It's going to start . . ."

Nicholas turned a bewildered look from one eager speaker to another.

"What are you all trying to say? One at a time, there. Let Otto talk. Otto, what's all this about a prize, and races, and the Squire?"

Otto drew a long, important breath, and began to talk fast so no one would interrupt him.

"There's going to be a big sled race on Christmas morning. All the boys are to start with their sleds at the Squire's gate at the top of the hill, and the first one who gets back to the big pine behind the Squire's vegetable garden on the other side of the house wins the prize — and — what is the prize? A big new sled . . ."

"With steel runners!" all the boys chorused delightedly.

"With steel runners!" echoed Nicholas in an awed whisper. "Go on, Otto. How are you supposed to go *up* a hill on a sled? And where else does the race go?"

Otto frowned at the others for silence, and continued. "Well, you coast down the long hill, and that will carry you across the frozen creek at the bottom. Then there's that patch of trees near the wood-cutter's cottage. Well, here's where the fun comes in. Every place you can't coast, you have to pull or carry your sled. There are about three fences to go over — the Groziks', the Bavrans', and the Pavlicks'; then you have to go through the Black Wood, where you know there are some clear, hilly stretches, and other places where you can't coast because of the trees. After you go through the wood, there's a long slide down to the village pasture; then you go back across the creek at the rapids, where it *isn't* frozen, then up the long hill behind the Squire's to the big pine. There, how's that for a race?"

Otto paused for breath triumphantly, and the others all started in again.

"Nicholas, you'll enter, won't you? That's not a bad sled you have, even if you did . . ."

"Hush, Jan," whispered another. "It isn't nice to

remind Nicholas that he made his own sled, just because our fathers had ours made for us."

But Nicholas was not listening to the conversation. He was thinking swiftly. Finally he turned to the others and asked, " What time does the race begin? "

" Nine o'clock sharp on Christmas morning," was the answer.

Nicholas shook his head doubtfully.

" I don't know whether I can be there," he said slowly. He was thinking of the chest full of toys he had planned to deliver to almost every house in the village. He had so many chores to do when he got up in the morning, that he didn't see how he could possibly finish his work, make his rounds with the gifts, and still be in time for the start of the race at nine o'clock.

The other boys looked at him, suddenly silenced by the thought that came to every mind. They knew what Nicholas was thinking of when he said he wasn't sure that he'd be there, and although every child had come to expect a toy from Nicholas on Christmas morning, these boys were too embarrassed to put into words the fact that because Nicholas was so good to them, and especially to their smaller brothers and sisters, he might not be able to enter this race, which was so exciting to every boy's heart. And for all his gentleness, Nicholas was a real boy, and felt the desire to enter this race and win the big sled with steel runners, just as much as any boy present.

"By getting up very early, and hurrying, I could get there," he was thinking. "If it only weren't for the doll I have to bring to Elsa, away outside the village . . . Oh, I have it!" his eyes gleamed with excitement. He suddenly remembered that Elsa's father was the wood-cutter, and that their cottage was right in the path of the race. The doll could easily be dropped off in a few seconds, and he could continue.

"I'll be there! I'll be there! At nine o'clock sharp, and then you'd better watch out for the prize," he shouted gleefully. "My old home-made sled may be heavy for the pulls and the places we have to carry, but that will make it all the faster on the coasts. I'll go by you just like this!"

And he made a lunge past little Josef Ornoff, which tumbled the astonished little fellow into a deep snowbank. All the other boys laughingly piled Nicholas in with Josef, and the whole meeting broke up in a fast and furious snow battle.

* * * * * * *

When the children of the village arose on Christmas morning, they found a bright sun streaming in through the cottage windows and gleaming on the hard crusted snow on the roads. But they also found that Nicholas had been there, and probably even before the sun, because every door-way in the village was heaped with the little toys — the result of a whole year's work. After the excitement over the gifts, all the boys made an anxious last-minute inspection of their sleds, made a trial run or two, and then the whole village started in a body for the starting-point of the race.

Nicholas, meanwhile, was back in his little shed, desperately working on a broken runner. It had collapsed at the last house under the strain of the extra-heavy burden of wooden toys, and even as Nicholas was feverishly lashing heavy bits of rope and twisted cord around the bottom of his sled, he could hear the faint echo of the horn from the Squire's house at the top of the hill, announcing the start of the race. He could have sobbed with disappointment, because he knew that he never could get there in time to start with the others, but he also realized he had to get to the wood-cutter's house anyway, so he turned the mended sled upright, and made a mad dash for the hilltop, where he found the villagers already looking excitedly after a group of black specks speeding down the hill, and shouting words of encouragement at the racers. As Nicholas panted his way through the crowd, they all made way for him, with loud expressions of sympathy that he hadn't arrived there in time.

"Come on, Nicholas lad," shouted Jan Bavran. "I vow I'd rather see you win than my own Otto. Here, men, let's give him a good push. One — two — three — off he goes!"

And down the hill sped Nicholas, his face and eyes stinging in the swift rush of wind, his hands cleverly steering the heavy sled which gained more and more speed so that the wooden runners seemed hardly to touch the packed snow. On and on he went, swifter and swifter; and now his eyes glowed with excitement as he saw that the boys' figures ahead of him were black specks no longer, and that he must have gained a good bit of ground.

Then, as the hill sloped more gently and the pace slackened, he noticed something ahead which puzzled him. The boys had all stopped on the other side of the frozen creek! Instead of going on through the patch of woods on the other side, they had, one and all, calmly alighted from their sleds, and were now standing stock-still, watching Nicholas approach. As his sled slowed down, and finally stopped, he looked bewilderedly from one to another, and started "What in the world . . ."

"Come on, Nicholas," spoke up little Josef; "we would have waited for you at the top, but the Squire got impatient and made us start when the horn blew. But of course you knew we'd wait for you."

"Yes," shouted Otto, "go throw that doll in Elsa's doorway, and then let's go! And from now on, see how long we'll wait for you! First come, first served with the sled with the steel runners!"

Nicholas put his hand on the nearest boy's shoulder. His eyes glistened with moisture, but it must have been from the sharp wind on the coast. He didn't say anything, but he was so happy at this boyish way of showing friendship that his heart was full.

Twenty boys delivered a doll to astonished little Elsa, and then, with a wild shout, they were off again, dragging their sleds after them, knocking against tree-trunks, getting their ropes tangled in low scrubby bushes, stumbling over rocks, climbing over fences, jumping on now and then for a stretch of coasting, bumping each other — laughing, excited, eager, happy boys!

And Nicholas was the happiest of all, even though his

sled was heavy to pull and clumsy to lift over fences. (His friends had waited for him!) Up would go the strong young arms and the sled was over the fence into the next field. (They *did* like him, even though he was an orphan and had no house of his own, but had to be passed around!) Over a steep grade he would drag the sled and then fling himself down for a wild rush. (And he had finished his morning's work too; every child in the village was playing with a toy Nicholas had made!) The long slide down to the village pasture with only one boy ahead of him! (I'll show them; I'll never let a Christmas pass without visiting every child in the village!) Now carrying the heavy sled on his shoulders while he felt slowly for a foothold on the flat stones of the part of the creek that was not frozen; he was the first boy to cross! (Up at the top of the hill, there's a beautiful sled with steel runners. It's big! It will hold twice as many toys as this old thing.) Up the hill, panting, hot, yellow locks flying in the wind, digging his toes in the hard snow, pulling for dear life at " the old thing," turning around excitedly once or twice to see how close the next boy was; then — suddenly, he heard the shouts of the villagers and he was at the top! He leaned against the big pine; he was home — he had won the race!

The big sled with steel runners was beautiful, but it was more beautiful still to see the defeated boys pulling Nicholas home on his prize, while the littler children hopped on behind and climbed lovingly all over the victor, and each mother and father smiled proudly as though it had been their own son who had won the race.

To talk about the special meaning of this chapter

turn to page 146

{ 24 }

CHAPTER 4
NIGHT BEFORE CHRISTMAS

FTER the crowd of villagers had dispersed on that merry Christmas Day of the race, Nicholas was stopped at the door of the fisherman's cottage he had lived in for a year, by a lean, dark-looking man who looked as though he had never smiled in his life. He had deep lines in his forehead, shaggy gray eyebrows which overhung and almost completely hid his deep-set gray eyes, and a mouth which went down at the corners, giving him an expression of grouchiness which never seemed to change. It was Bertran Marsden, the wood-carver of the village, and all the children called him Mad Marsden, because he lived alone, spoke to hardly anybody in the town, and chased the children away from his door with black looks and harsh words.

He now edged up to Nicholas, who was busy dragging his beloved new sled to his work-shed behind the house.

"You haven't forgotten, Nicholas, that you move to my house today," Marsden said gruffly.

Nicholas looked up. No, he had not forgotten, and he well knew why Marsden had offered to take him in for the last year of his life as a wandering orphan. The old wood-carver had no children for Nicholas to take care of, he did no farming or fishing, and therefore did not need a boy to help him out in that direction. The only reason he was willing, even eager, to feed and clothe the orphan was because for almost five years now he had watched the work Nicholas had been doing with his knife and carved woods, and realized that he could get a good apprentice cheap, without paying even a cent for the good work he knew he could get out of him.

Knowing all these things, and thinking of the bleak little cottage he would have to live in for a year, where there was no laughter and sound of children's voices, it was with a heavy heart that Nicholas piled up his few belongings in the new sled, said a grateful farewell to the family he was leaving, and followed Mad Marsden home to the low, mean-looking cottage on the outskirts of the village.

On entering the cottage, he stepped immediately into the main workroom of the wood-carver. Here were found his bench, his table, his tools, and his woods. A broad fireplace almost filled another side of the room, and black pots and greasy kettles showed plainly that no scouring housewife had set foot in the cottage for years. A pile of tumbled blankets in one corner was evidently Marsden's bed, and near the window was a table, littered with the remains of his morning meal. These and a few rickety chairs completed the furnishings of this one dark room.

Marsden led the way in and pointed to a door in the corner.

"You can stow your belongings in there," he said over his shoulder to Nicholas, who was standing in the middle of the untidy room, looking around him in dismay. "There's a cot you can sleep on, and you may as well put that pretty sled away for good. We have no time here to go romping in the snow."

Nicholas nodded silently, too puzzled at the old man's living quarters to be hurt by the harsh words. He could not understand why Marsden should live so meanly, because, as the only wood-carver in the village, he was kept busy all the time filling orders for his hand-carved tables, chairs, cabinets, bridal chests, sleighs, and several other useful household articles that the villagers were in constant need of. The poorer people paid him in flour, vegetables, fish — whatever they could send him; the more well-to-do gave him good gold coin for his work. Not only that, but it was a well-known fact that he did work for the people in two or three neighboring villages, where there was no other wood-carver. In spite of the fact, then, that he probably had more money than any of the poor fishermen in the village, his cottage was meaner and shabbier than any of the well-scrubbed houses in which Nicholas had spent the past nine years.

"Come now, Nicholas, don't stand there gawking. Put away your belongings; you have much to learn here. I'm going to make a good wood-carver of you. No time for silly little dolls and wooden horses; you'll have to earn your keep here. And mind you, I won't have this place filled with screaming little brats. You keep that tribe of young ones that's always following you about out of here, do you understand?"

His eyes gleamed fiercely beneath the shaggy brows. Nicholas stammered in a frightened voice, "Yes — yes, master. But," he pleaded, suddenly struck by the thought that he might not see any of his little friends any more, " but they don't do any harm, the children — they only like to watch me work, and I wouldn't let them get in your way or touch anything . . ."

"Silence!" roared the old man, shaking his fists in the air and glaring at the frightened boy. "I won't have 'em, do you understand? I want to be alone. I wouldn't have you here if the work didn't pile up so that I need a helper. But you'll have to work, and there'll be no time for Christmas visits to children and all that nonsense."

Nicholas bowed his head and went silently to work putting away his small bundle of clothing, his few books, his father's sea-chest and jack-knife. The year ahead of him stretched forth bleakly, and only the thought that he was now fourteen years old and almost a man kept him from crying himself to sleep that night in his dark, cold little room.

So Nicholas started to work for the mad old wood-carver, and learned many things. He learned that his father's old jack-knife was a clumsy tool compared with the beautiful sharp knives and wheels that Marsden used; he learned to work for hours, bent over the bench beside his master, patiently going over and over one stick of wood until it was planed to the exact hundredth of an inch that his teacher required; he learned to keep on working even though the back of his neck almost shrieked with pain, and the muscles of his arms and hands grew lame from so much steady labor. All this he grew used to in time, for he was a strong, sturdy lad, and young enough so that his muscles became accustomed to the hard work; but what he felt he never could get used to was the dreadful loneliness of the place. His friends, the children, gradually gave up trying to see him after they had been shooed away from the door by the cross old wood-carver; Marsden himself rarely talked, except to give brief instructions about the work, or to scold him for some mistake. So Nicholas was sad and lonely, and longed for the days when he had been in friendly cottages, surrounded by a laughing group of children.

In addition to his duties at the work-bench, he also attempted to straighten out the two miserable little rooms where they lived. Marsden was surprised one morning on awakening to discover that Nicholas, who had risen two hours earlier, had swept and scrubbed the floor and hearth-stone, taken down the dirty hangings from the two little windows and had them airing in the yard, and was now busily scrubbing with clean sea-sand the dirt-incrusted pots and pans. The table was set in front of the fire with a clean white cloth and dishes, and the kettle was bubbling merrily on the hearth.

Marsden opened his mouth to speak.

Marsden opened his mouth to speak, then closed it without saying a word. Nicholas took the kettle from the fire, poured the boiling water over the tea-leaves, spread some bread with fresh, sweet butter, and said simply, " Your breakfast, master."

Marsden ate wordlessly, looking at Nicholas from under his wild eyebrows. The boy went on with his work, which consisted now in bundling up the tumbled bed-clothing and throwing it over a line in the yard. Marsden finished his breakfast and finally spoke.

" You'll find some meal in that corner cupboard," he said. " We might have some porridge tomorrow morning." Nicholas nodded. " Now, stop all that woman's work and let's get on with that chest. I've promised it for next Wednesday, and even if that silly Enid Grondin is fool enough to get married, we must have our work out when it is promised."

But after that morning, Marsden was careful to shake out his bed-clothing after he arose, and to clean up the dishes after his breakfast. And the cottage gradually came to look more like a place where human beings could live.

One night, as Marsden sat in front of his fire, silently smoking his long pipe, he noticed that Nicholas was still bent over the work-bench.

{ 32 }

"Here, lad," he said almost kindly, in his gruff voice, "I'm not such a hard master that I have you work night as well as day. What's that you're doing? Why don't you go to your bed, hey?"

Nicholas answered hastily. "It's just a piece of wood you threw away, master, and I thought I'd see if I could copy that fine chair you made for Mistress Grozik. This is a little one — a toy," he ended fearfully; for he well knew that the word "toy" would mean children to old Marsden, and for some strange reason just to mention a child in his presence sent him into a rage.

Tonight, however, he contented himself with merely a black look, and said, "Let me see it. Hmm — not bad, but you have that scroll on the back bigger on one side than the other. Here, give me that knife."

Nicholas hastened with the tool, and watched admiringly as the old wood-carver deftly corrected the mistake.

"There," Marsden said finally, holding his work away from him, "that's the way it should be done."

Then, instead of handing the little chair to Nicholas, who was waiting expectantly, he continued holding it in his hands, while a bitter and yet rather sad expression came into the fierce old eyes, and a smile, — Nicholas blinked and looked again, — yes, a real smile was tugging at the corners of that stern mouth which had been turned down for so many years.

"It's a long time since I made one of these wee things," he murmured half to himself. "Yet I made plenty, years and years ago, when they were little."

Nicholas ventured a timid question. "When who were little, master?"

The corners of Marsden's mouth went down again; his eyes turned fierce and angry once more. "My sons," he roared. "I once had two sons, and when they were as big as you, they ran away to sea, and left me all alone, left me to grow old and crabbed, so the children call me Mad Marsden. Children, bah! Do you wonder why I'll have none of them around my house? Do you wonder when I can't stand their baby voices babbling around here, where once . . ." His voice broke, and he buried his old head in his hands.

Nicholas wasn't afraid of him any more; he went over and put his pitying young hands on the old shoulders. "I'll be your son, master; I won't leave you," he whispered.

Marsden lifted his head, and looked at the strong young face with the kind blue eyes bent over him. "You're a good lad, Nicholas. And," he added almost shyly, for it

"It's a long time since I made one of these wee things."

wasn't easy for a harsh man to change so quickly, " I think I'd like to help you with some of those little things you make. We'll make them together these long winter evenings, eh, shall we, Nicholas? So you can go around next Christmas Day in that fine sled of yours. Then you won't leave me alone again, will you, lad?"

He grasped Nicholas' arm almost roughly, then a peaceful expression crept into the lonely old face as the boy answered simply, " No, master, I'll stay here with you just as long as you want me."

So every winter evening saw two heads bent over the work-bench — a gray head with thick, shaggy hair, and the smooth yellow head of the boy. They worked feverishly during the weeks preceding Christmas; and with the old man helping with the carving, Nicholas was able to add delicate little touches to the toys which made them far more handsome than any he had ever made before. He painted the dolls' faces so that their eyes were as blue and their cheeks and lips were as rosy as the little girls who would soon clasp them in their arms; the little chairs and tables were stained with the same soft colors that Marsden used on his own products; the little boys' sleighs and boats and animals were shiny with bright new paints, — red and yellow and green.

So, two nights before Christmas, everything was finished, — a toy for every child in the village was packed in the sled with the steel runners; yet Nicholas and the old man were still working at the bench. This time, they were desperately trying to finish a chest which had been ordered by a wealthy woman in the next village, twenty miles away. She had said definitely that she wanted the chest finished in time for Christmas Day, because she was giving it to her daughter as a betrothal gift and the feast was to be celebrated then. Marsden and Nicholas worked feverishly most of that night and the following day, and there still remained a few little finishing touches, and here it was Christmas Eve. Marsden could have it done in time to be delivered tomorrow, but of course Nicholas would have to borrow the nearest neighbor's horse and drive over with the chest on Christmas Day itself, — the day when he had planned to make his tour of the village with his gifts, to show the children that he had not forgotten them, even though they had not seen much of him during the past year.

"I'm sorry, Nicholas," said old Marsden. "I'd go myself, but I'm not as strong as I used to be, and it's an all-day trip — twenty miles over, then you'll have to wait several hours to rest the horse, and twenty miles back. And with the snow not crusted, it'll be hard going."

Nicholas was sitting in front of the fire, leaning on his elbows, staring thoughtfully into the flames.

"If she only didn't want the chest tomorrow for sure," he said. "And if we had only finished it before today, I could have delivered it sooner, and had plenty of time tomorrow."

"Well," answered his master, "we did promise it, and it has to be delivered. Now the toys weren't promised . . ."

"No, but I always have given them," interrupted Nicholas.

"I was just going to say, lad, that they weren't promised for Christmas *Day*. Now, you know that little children go to bed early. Why can't you . . ."

"Oh, I understand," cried Nicholas, leaping from his chair. "I deliver the gifts tonight, Christmas Eve, after the children have gone to bed, and when they wake up tomorrow morning, they'll find them there, at their doors! Oh, master, that's a wonderful idea! Why, it's even better than before. I never did like the idea of walking up to a house in broad daylight and hearing people thank me and

{ 38 }

everything. What time is it, quick? Eleven o'clock! I'll have to hurry. Where's my list? Where's my sled? "

So the two rushed around and finally got the sled out in the yard. Nicholas bundled himself up in his close-fitting hat shaped like a stocking, his long belted tunic coat edged with fur, his black leggings and heavy boots, pulled on his mittens, and was off through the snow, dragging the toy-laden sled behind him.

Christmas Eve in the village — a bright winter moon shining in the star-filled sky; glistening white snow banked everywhere — on the roads, on the roof-tops, on the fences, and in the doorways; houses darkened and the inmates all sleeping soundly; not a soul stirring in the streets but one figure, which stole silently from door to door, leaving a pile of tiny objects every place he stopped, until there was nothing left in the bottom of the sled. It was three o'clock on Christmas morning when Nicholas turned away from the last doorway, his sled lighter to pull, his feet tired from dragging through the heavy snow, but happy that it was Christmas morning and he had once more kept his unspoken promise to the children.

To talk about the special meaning of this chapter

turn to page 146

{ 39 }

CHAPTER 5
THE WOOD-CARVER

ICHOLAS did not leave the wood-carver on Christmas Day, or the next year, or the next. He stayed on in the little cottage, which was now bright and clean, and a happy dwelling for two happy people. For old Marsden had forgotten his grouch in the daily association with Nicholas' sunny disposition; he cheerfully taught Nicholas all he knew of his difficult trade, so that as the boy grew in years and strength, his knowledge of wood-carving soon matched that of his old master. Marsden bought a horse and sleigh for the trips outside of town, which were also used by Nicholas on his Christmas Eve visits to the children in the village. For although the little ones he had played with had grown up and stopped playing with toys, there were new babies in every household every year, and each one was taught to expect from Nicholas, the wood-carver, a little toy on Christmas morning.

One bright summer morning, Nicholas was sitting on a bench outside the cottage door, carving away at a half-finished chair leg and whistling cheerfully as he worked. He was then twenty years old, a tall young man, the yellow hair a little darker, but with the same blue eyes, rosy cheeks, and ready smile. He stopped his work to listen to the birds singing in the trees overhead and to enjoy the warm sunlight shining down on him. Suddenly two children ran up the path leading to the cottage door, bursting with news.

" Nicholas," one of them panted, " Nicholas, there are two men in the village who have been asking where old Marsden lives. They are on their way here now. Who do you suppose they are? They said . . . "

" Hush," said the other child, " here they are now."

Two men, about ten or fifteen years older than Nicholas, were coming slowly up the path. They seemed surprised to see him working at the bench, and one of them spoke.

" Excuse me, but they told us in the village that we would find Bertran Marsden here. If we have made a mistake, . . . "

" No," answered Nicholas, " this is Bertran Marsden's

cottage. I am only his apprentice. I'll call him. He has a nap every afternoon now. You see, he's getting rather old."

The two men looked at each other with shamed eyes.

" Yes, he must be old now. Don't disturb him. We'll come back."

" No, here he is now," said Nicholas.

Marsden had appeared in the doorway and was looking from one to the other with puzzled eyes.

One of the men stepped forward. " Father," he began.

" Father! " Marsden tottered a little; Nicholas put out a steadying arm.

" Yes, don't you remember us, Father? I am Henrik and this is Lons. We left you years ago, but we finally made our fortune and are ready to take you home."

" Take me home! " Old Marsden straightened himself. " This is my home, and you are two strange men to me."

" No, Father," answered Lons. " We are your two sons. We are sorry we left you alone years ago, but boys are thoughtless, and we wanted only the adventure and didn't think how much we might be hurting you. If you'll forgive us now, . . . "

The old man looked at his two sons for a long moment.

"Yes, of course I'll forgive you. If you had come back a few years ago, I couldn't have done it. I have found another son. This is Nicholas, who lives with me, and who does most of my work now."

The sons looked at Nicholas, then back at their father again, uncertain how to go on. Finally Henrik spoke.

"We've just bought a house in the next village, Father. Lons and I have a fishing boat there, and we're doing well. We want you to come there and live with us. We want to make up to you for the years we were away."

Marsden shook his head. "No, my lads; I have my little cottage here, and Nicholas helps me with my work. I don't need anything, and I couldn't live without working."

Lons answered quickly. "But you could go on working in our village, Father. There's no wood-carver there, and if you insist, there are many people who would give you something to do. We so want to have you; we've been planning all through our travels how, when we came home again, we'd take care of you and live with you and make you forget that we were ever heedless boys who ran away for an adventure. And Nicholas here, — why, he could easily take over the business in this village, if he's as good as you say. He's young, and probably ambitious; why don't you give him a chance, Father?"

None of the arguments seemed to make much impression on the old man until the end; then he listened attentively and paused a while before he spoke.

"Yes," he said slowly. "Nicholas deserves something like this. He could do it easily. He's a bright lad . . . "

Nicholas interrupted. "Don't think of me, master. If you don't want to go with them, we'll go on living here together just the same as before. I don't want to take your business."

"There, lad," said Marsden, laying a hand on Nicholas' shoulder, "I don't want to leave you either, but you're young, and youth should be given a chance. Besides," he paused, and looked at the two tall men standing before him, as anxious and nervous as boys, their eyes pleading silently with their father, "besides, these are my own sons, and I think they need me as much as I need them."

Henrik and Lons sprang over to the old man's side.

"Father, does it mean you will . . . "

Marsden nodded his head, grown almost white in the last few years. "Yes, I'll just move along to the next village with you, my sons, and I'll leave this cottage and my tools with my other son, Nicholas."

He put a loving hand on Nicholas' shoulder, and then the four went inside the house to discuss how and when the move would be made.

A week later, Nicholas found himself the owner of a two-room cottage, a perfect set of wood-carver's tools, and a well-established business which should keep him housed, fed, and clothed for life. At first he was lonely in the little cottage after Marsden had left with his sons, but he soon became interested in his work, which kept him so busy he had no time to feel alone. Then, too, there was almost always a child or two chatting to him or playing with its toys on the cottage floor.

Nicholas divided his day now so that he spent only part of his time on the orders he received; the rest of the day and most of the evenings he worked on toys for the next Christmas; for he now had such a long list of children it took months to complete the set of gifts he had to make.

He continued his practice, established the year he had to deliver the chest on Christmas Day, of making his rounds on Christmas Eve; and one year, he was considerably surprised and touched to see that the children had hung on their doors little embroidered bags filled with oats for his horse. So now, instead of leaving the toys piled up in the doorway, he put them in the little bags.

So it was a busy, happy existence that Nicholas led in the little wood-carver's cottage on the outskirts of the village, and as he grew older, the sound of children's voices lifted in their play became dearer and dearer to him; and the children, in their turn, loved to be near the tall, kind man with the light-colored beard whom everybody called Nicholas, the wood-carver.

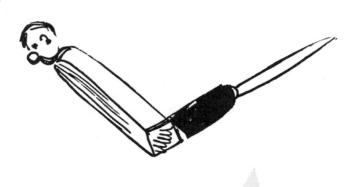

 **To talk about the special meaning of this chapter**

turn to page 147

CHAPTER 6
FIRST CHRISTMAS STOCKING

AURENS and Friedrik were two little newcomers in the village. Their mother and father were even poorer than most of the other families, which made them poor indeed, because nobody in the village had a great deal of money. Ever since the day of their arrival, they had been met by misfortune. Their father was a fisherman and used to be able to keep his family supplied with enough food to eat and enough fuel to keep them warm; but one day his boat had been caught in a storm, and the heavy mast had fallen on him, paralyzing him so that he had been forced to stay in bed and watch his little family grow thinner and thinner from lack of enough food to eat.

Their neighbors gave them as much of their meager supplies as they themselves could spare, and the mother worked occasionally in the household of the Squire or some of the more well-to-do families of the village, but there were still many meals in the little cottage which consisted solely of a piece of dried bread or fish, or a dish of thin gruel.

Laurens was now the man of the family, although he was only eight years old. He built fires, shoveled the heavy snow from the cottage door, kept the house neat and clean while his mother was out working, and took care of his little brother Friedrik. One of his principal duties was going into the forest and helping the wood-cutter, receiving in return for this service enough wood to keep his family supplied with fuel. He rather enjoyed this task, for he met many of the other boys while he was out. Although he worked while they played, he enjoyed being with children his own age after long hours spent in the house with his sick father and four-year-old brother.

One cold winter afternoon, as he was returning from the forest with his sled piled with the wood he had helped cut, he met a merry group of boys who were building a snow fort a few hundred yards away from the cottage of Nicholas, the wood-carver.

One of the boys noticed the little figure dragging the heavy sled and called out, " Ho there, Laurens! Want to be on our side? "

Laurens paused and looked wistfully at the boys playing in the snow. "I guess not," he answered. "I ought to get this wood home before nightfall."

"Oh, you have plenty of time," one of them replied. "There's a good hour yet before the sun goes down, and we'll help you drag your wood if you'll stay."

Laurens hesitated, then dropped the rope of his sled and joined the group. After all, his mother was home that afternoon, so his father and Friedrik would be taken care of, and there was enough fuel in the house to keep the fire going until evening. And it was a long time since he had played in the snow. So for a merry, carefree hour he forgot the troubles and duties of his house, and was only an eight-year-old boy having a good time. When it was his turn to storm the fort, he joined his side, and with breathless, gay courage, braved the storm of snowballs, climbed the icy walls of the fort, and took noisy possession. Then it was his turn to help his comrades hold the fort, so he warily kept out of sight, watching his chance to rise now and then above the white edge of the stronghold and hurl snowy missiles at the oncoming foe, and pausing every once in a while to make himself a new supply of ammunition.

It was during one of these moments, while he was busy

collecting snow and packing it into firm round balls, that he heard a glad shout from both sides, from his comrades inside the fort and his enemies outside, — " Nicholas! Hey, fellows, here's Nicholas! " — and looked up to see the tall figure of the wood-carver approaching the group. As he came nearer, he lifted his mittened hand to wave to the boys; his rosy, kindly face beaming a welcome, his blue eyes twinkling at the sight of the good time everybody seemed to be having.

" Well, well, a snow-fight! " he said in his deep voice. " It's a long time since I've had one of them; and when I was a boy, we knew how to take a fort. Now, I'd go about it like this."

He stooped swiftly and gathered up a handful of snow, and quickly packing and shaping it in his hands, took the finished snowball, and threw it with sure, accurate aim at the tallest boy behind the fort. It knocked the surprised fellow's hat clean off, and the other side, delighted with this new ally, rushed forward, Nicholas in their midst, and took the fort amid loud shouts and hurrahs.

Laurens looked at the tall man shyly. Of course he knew who Nicholas was; he had heard of him ever since his family had moved into the village last summer. He knew

"Well, well, a snow-fight!"

that he was the man who kept the children supplied with toys and gifts on Christmas Day, but of course he also supposed that Nicholas only remembered the children he really knew.

The snow-party started to break up then, as most of the boys had to be home before nightfall, and the sun was already sinking in the west. They started towards home then, accompanying Nicholas as far as his cottage. At the gate, the wood-carver paused a moment, looking over the group with keen eyes that seemed to see everything.

"Is this a new boy in the village?" he asked, laying a hand on Laurens' shoulder, and looking down kindly into the shy brown eyes.

"Yes, his name is Laurens, and he has a little brother Friedrik . . ."

"And his father is paralyzed, and doesn't work, and his mother . . ."

One of the boys dug his elbow sharply into the side of the last speaker.

"Now you've done it," he said angrily. "Why can't you hold your tongue? You've hurt his feelings by talking about his family right out like that. Here, I'm going after him. Come on, fellows."

And they ran after Laurens, leaving Nicholas alone at the gate, with a wise smile on his lips and a knowing shake of his head.

The group finally caught up with Laurens, who furtively wiped his eyes and mumbled something about having to be home anyway. The boys tried to distract his attention from the thoughtless remarks by talking about the man they had just left.

" That's Nicholas, the wood-carver, he's wonderful," volunteered one boy. " Every Christmas now, at least ever since I can remember, he's been leaving gifts at the doors in the village."

" Not every door," said another. " He only leaves them at the houses where he sees an embroidered bag. My mother told me that since the village has grown, Nicholas doesn't know every child the way he used to, so how does he know which house has children and which hasn't unless there's a bag there? "

" Yes," chimed in another, " and how would he even know how many gifts to leave unless there was a bag for each one? "

So they went on and on about the wonderful things Nicholas gave them, quite forgetting little Laurens, trudging along with his heavy sled, and his heart growing just as heavy with each step.

When he reached home, his mind was still occupied with the information he had heard that afternoon. It would be wonderful for little Friedrik to have a gift from that kind man. Of course, it did not matter so much about him; he was eight years old and didn't mind — at least, not *very* much — if he didn't get a toy; because when in the world would he have time to play with toys? But the problem that began to spin round and round in his head was, — how could he fix it so that Nicholas would know there was a little boy in their house?

That night he tried to get his mother interested.

"Mother," he began somewhat doubtfully, for he well knew how tired she must be, and probably unwilling to listen to nonsense about Christmas toys when her mind was occupied with the problem of where the next meal was coming from. "Mother, do you suppose we have a bag in the house?"

"A bag! What kind of bag, child?" she asked, astonished.

"Well, it should be an embroidered bag, really, but I suppose any kind of bag would do. You hang it outside the door Christmas Eve, and then when Friedrik wakes up the next morning, there's a fine toy for him. It's Nicholas, the wood-carver, who does it, and I thought that if there was only some kind of a bag around here . . . "

The mother sighed. "Things like potatoes and flour come in bags, child, and those are things we haven't seen for many days. And goodness knows, with all my worries, I have no time to make you one. Forget about this Nicholas person anyway," she finished bitterly. "I don't suppose he'd come to poor children like you, anyway."

So Laurens was forced to abandon the idea of a bag to hang outside the door for Friedrik's Christmas gift, but he couldn't forget about Nicholas. Why, out there in the forest, he looked like such a kind, jolly man; he wouldn't pass by a child's house just because he was poor. He thought and thought, until finally Christmas Eve arrived. He was sitting by the fire helping his little brother to undress. He sat staring into the fire while Friedrik capered around in his little night-shirt, taking advantage of his big brother's thoughtful moment to play just one more minute before going to bed. Laurens absent-mindedly began to make a neat pile of the little fellow's clothing so it would be ready for him in the morning. As he picked up a little stocking, long and warm and woolly, he held it up, and said jokingly, "Now, that would hold some kind of gift, just as well as any embroidered bag . . . "

He stopped short, and stared intently at the stocking. "Why not?" he murmured, half to himself. "Why not?"

Little Friedrik looked frightened. "Laurens, Laurens, what are you looking at my stocking for? What are you going to do with it?"

Laurens gave a joyful shout. "Do with it? I'm going to hang it outside the door!" and with one leap, he flung open the cottage door.

* * * * * * *

Christmas Eve in the village — a bright winter moon shining in the star-filled sky — glistening, white snow banked everywhere — on the roads, on the rooftops, on the fences, and in the doorways; houses darkened and inmates all sleeping soundly; not a soul stirring in the streets but one figure, which stole silently from door to door, leaving bulging bags filled with gifts. At Laurens' doorway the figure paused. In the bright moonlight, there was a funny object to be seen dangling outside the door — a child's woolen stocking! Nicholas laughed silently, a kind, tender

{ 56 }

There was a funny object seen dangling outside the door.

laugh, then reached down into his pack and filled the lonely little stocking to the top. And with a snap of his whip and a jingling of sleighbells, he was off to the next house.

The next morning, little Friedrik was presented with not one, nor two, but five tiny little toys — boats and horses and sleighs; and in the bottom of the stocking, way down in the toe, were five large pieces of gold, enough to keep a whole family through the winter. Little Friedrik shouted with joy, the father almost sat up in bed in his excitement, the mother's eyes were bright with happy tears, and Laurens hugged close to his heart the first Christmas stocking.

To talk about the special meaning of this chapter

turn to page 148

CHAPTER 7
NICHOLAS' FIRST RED SUIT

QUIRE KENSON, the richest man in the village, came driving up to Nicholas' cottage door one day, with a commission to carve a new chest for his youngest daughter, who was planning to be married. Nicholas was attracted by the sound of silver bells and reindeer's hoofs on the snow; he looked out of his window and saw the beautiful equipage the Squire traveled about in, — a shiny, red sleigh, drawn by two beautiful reindeer — Donder and Blitzen they were called by the children of the village, because they traveled so swiftly, like thunder and lightning. Nicholas gazed at the two beautiful animals and thought how much more rapidly they would carry him about on Christmas Eve than his old horse, who was getting slower and slower as the years went on.

Then Nicholas hastened to open the door for the Squire,

who stated his errand briefly and gave directions about the size of the chest and when he expected it to be finished. All the while he was talking, the wood-carver was gazing admiringly at the fine suit of red deerskin his visitor was wearing. As he nodded and made notes of the instructions, his eyes missed no detail of the Squire's outfit; the suit was made in the fashion of the district — that is, the coat rather long and belted at the waist, the trousers loose and caught in at the calf by shining leather leggings. Soft, white ermine bound the coat at the collar, the cuffs, and around the bottom; the same beautiful fur was around the close-fitting red hat.

After the Squire had finished his errand, and had driven off, led by Donder and Blitzen's flying hoofs, Nicholas went on with the task in hand, but with his mind on the beautiful red suit.

"There's no reason why I can't have one, too," he said to himself. "I have all my winter supplies in and the wood all paid for, and there is still a bag of gold coin that I will never be able to spend. The Widow Arpen could well make use of some of it, and they say that she is the cleverest needlewoman in the village. I think I'll drive over there tomorrow and see what can be done. I've gone around looking like a poor orphan instead of a well-to-do wood-carver long enough."

So the next day Nicholas paid a visit to Widow Arpen's cottage.

"I want a fine red suit, Mistress Arpen," he stated. "You know the one the Squire wears?" The woman nodded. "Well, of course, I can't afford such fine, soft deerskin; besides, there's no time to have all that skin dressed and prepared; and I know very well I can't have mine trimmed with real ermine. Now what could you suggest?"

The widow thought a moment. "Well," she said finally, "we could get a good bolt of strong homespun from the weaver, and I could dye it myself. I have had a wonderful red from stewing rowan berries. Then I'm sure we could get enough pure white rabbit skins from Lief the trapper to trim the neck and cuffs. It would make a fine suit, and you'd look splendid in it, Nicholas."

Nicholas rose, well pleased with the plan for the work. He took out of his pocket a handful of gold coins and laid them on the table.

"There," he said, "I think that will take care of the material and the labor."

"But — but, Nicholas, it's more than enough!" the

widow exclaimed. " Why, half of this would keep my family all through the winter."

" Then keep it, woman," smiled Nicholas. " You've had a hard time since your good man died to keep your little family warm and well fed. I have enough and to spare, so let's not quibble over a few gold coins. I'll not be the man to die with a chest of them found buried under my hearth-stone."

The widow stood at her door and watched Nicholas drive away through the snow. " Eh, there's a fine man," she murmured, the gold pieces jingling through her fingers. " A fine, big man."

So she bought the homespun, which she dyed a beautiful bright red. And then a strange thing happened. She had no pattern to go by, as Nicholas was wearing the only tunic he owned, and could spare no time from his work to have a fitting, so the widow cut and sewed the suit with the image of a fine, big man constantly before her. Nicholas was not a short man by any means, but he was rather thin, and yet as Mistress Arpen planned and pieced the suit together, she knew she was sewing for a fine, generous man, and made the suit to fit Nicholas' heart instead of his body.

On the day the work was finished, and the last loving

stitch had been placed in the soft rabbit trimming, Nicholas arrived to try on his suit. He went into the widow's little inner room, and came out a few minutes later — and what a picture he made!

"I can't see it, Mistress Arpen," said Nicholas doubtfully, "for that little piece of glass in your room shows only a portion of me at a time. Yet it did seem to go on rather — rather loosely," he finished tactfully, not wishing to hurt her feelings.

The widow gave one look and burst into tears. "Oh, Nicholas, I've spoiled your suit; I've spoiled it! I thought you were bigger; whatever made me cut it so wide? Oh, what shall I do?"

Trying to comfort the woman, Nicholas forgot his own dismay at the size of his garments.

"There, we won't worry about it. Look, the length is all right. It's only that I'm not as fat as I might be. Why if I ate all the vegetables and meal the villagers send me, I'll warrant in a few months' time you'd never notice the extra cloth in this coat. And the trousers will be all right as soon as I buy a pair of leggings to stuff them in. And what a fine cap this is! See how close it fits, and how warm-looking this fur band is!"

"I'm not as fat as I might be."

So gradually he made the widow forget her disappointment, and to reassure her that he really did not mind the ludicrous figure he must make with his tall, gangly form clothed in loose, baggy folds, he insisted on wearing it home, and sat up high on the seat of his sleigh and seemed not to notice the stares and nudges of the villagers.

When he arrived home, however, he sat down in the huge suit and burst into loud laughter. " What a sight I'll make going around like this for months to come! And yet I'll have to wear it out; it would be sinful to waste good material."

Then another funny thought struck him. He slapped his knee and laughed again. " Perhaps I could even stuff some of my toys into my suit. How the children would laugh! But there's only one thing to be done. It's very clear that I'm too thin for my height. I shall really have to eat oatmeal in the morning instead of just a piece of bread; and I must drink more milk, and cook some of those vegetables that go to waste in the storeroom."

So Nicholas kept his big red suit, and soon the villagers became used to the tall figure in the bright red trousers and tunic, the close-fitting stocking-cap trimmed with white fur, and the shiny black leather belt and leggings. And what

"I shall really have to eat oatmeal in the morning."

the cottage for more gifts. He loaded the sleigh again and started out once more, with the night half gone and his list not completed.

Poor old Lufka, his horse, tried his best, but he was getting old and could not make very fast progress through the heavy snow. He kept turning a patient head around at Nicholas, who spoke to him encouragingly. " Come on, now, lad; only two more houses. You can make it; the sleigh's not so heavy now with all that double load delivered."

Lufka wagged his head at his master's voice and tossed it in the air as though to say, " Yes, but tonight we had to make an extra trip back to the cottage, and when I thought I was going to be nicely bedded down for the night, off you went again! And I must say I like the snow better when there's a crust on top, instead of this heavy stuff. I'm always stumbling — there, now!"

Down went the good old beast into a ditch, and crack went one of the sleigh runners. Nicholas climbed down, and after reassuring himself that Lufka had no broken bones, shook his head ruefully at the sight of the old sleigh.

" I guess that's the end of that, old boy," he remarked to Lufka, who had stumbled upright and was now busy trying to flick the snow off with his tail. "Looks as though we'll have to get a new sleigh, and I'm afraid your traveling days are over, too. You're getting a little old for this heavy driving."

Nicholas had to finish his Christmas visits on foot, and the first rosy streaks of dawn were brightening the sky when he and Lufka finally returned to the cottage, — Nicholas, fat and rosy, puffing heavily; Lufka dragging his tired old bones straight to the door of his stable.

For many days after that particular Christmas Eve, the villagers and children who passed Nicholas' door noticed that he was not working at his bench. Instead, there could be heard sounds of hammering and sawing from the large shed where he kept his supply of wood and where he did the larger pieces of work which required more room.

The villagers said to each other, "Must be some beautiful bridal chest that keeps Nicholas so busy these days. Or maybe it's a boat he's building for himself," they joked.

Spring came, the late northern spring, and Nicholas was again seen at his work-bench. When curious townsfolk questioned him on his long, secret task of the winter, he would only shake his dark yellow head (the yellow was now beginning to show streaks of white) and say with a sly smile, " You'll see soon enough. Just you wait."

Soon, however, the villagers forgot their curiosity in a new, exciting piece of news which was spreading over the village. Nicholas heard most of it at his work-bench, where people of all ages gathered now and then to chat with the wood-carver.

" What's this I hear about the Squire, Otto? " Nicholas asked his old friend, with whom he had lived as a boy.

" Ah," said Otto, puffing contentedly at his pipe and settling down to a long gossip. " They say things haven't gone so well with him these past five years or more. First there were those ships of his that didn't come home; then they say that his overseer ran away with a good part of a year's rents . . ."

" Yes," put in old Hans Klinker, " then there was that matter of a mine that his son persuaded him to invest in."

" Too bad," they all sighed, with a sort of self-satisfied air that they would have done nothing so foolish with *their* money, if they had ever had any to be foolish with.

" And now," continued Otto, leaning forward with the most interesting part of his story, " now he has to sell most of his lands and household goods to pay the creditors and

{ 71 }

start in again. Will you be going up to the sale tomorrow, Nicholas? "

Nicholas looked up from the piece of wood he was planing, to ask, " Now what would I be buying from the Squire? I don't want any more land, and I can make for myself as fine furniture as any he has in his house."

" He has some good animals up there," said old Hans. " Those two horses now, and that set of reindeer."

" True enough," said Nicholas, finally interested enough to put down his work. " Lufka's too old to be much help to me now. I think I might go up there with you boys tomorrow and see some of the excitement."

So the next morning found Nicholas in the center of an eager, curious crowd — farmers who hoped to get some of the Squire's good land cheap; fishermen who were interested in the two or three boats the Squire owned; housewives who thought they might like a chair or a table from such a fine household; and scores of others who had come along just to watch the rest of the crowd.

Nicholas wandered down to the stables, and was instantly surrounded by a group of men who knew he was interested in horses and were ready to give him much free advice.

Nicholas, however, walked past the stables where the horses were lodged, and made directly for the larger stalls.

"He's after Donder and Blitzen," the men whispered among themselves. "He always admired them, they went so fast."

Yes, there was Nicholas, his round figure in the bright red suit standing at the door of the stable, his hands on his roomy hips, gazing thoughtfully in at the darkened stalls. Two deer, inside, excited at the noises of the crowd, thrust their frightened heads through the top part of the door.

"Well," said Nicholas softly, "you poor beasties don't look much like thunder and lightning now. Not afraid of me, are you?" He put a reassuring hand on the larger deer's shoulder. The melting brown eyes looked trustingly into the blue ones. The deer whimpered and thrust its warm black nose into Nicholas' hand.

"I guess we'll get along all right," said Nicholas in a satisfied tone. "Now to find your master and see about this sale."

"Here's the Squire now," called out one of the men. "Nicholas wants to buy Donder and Blitzen, Squire."

The Squire, a bent old man with a worried look on his

face, seemed dazed by this mob of people taking possession of his house and goods.

"Well, he can't have Donder and Blitzen, alone," he said almost fretfully. "That set of reindeer goes together or not at all. Why, Donder would go raving mad if you tried to separate her from the rest of her family."

"Family!" exclaimed Nicholas. "Why, Squire, I need only two reindeer. How many more . . ."

Suddenly there was a loud crash of breaking wood, a mad rush of people away from one of the stalls, and seemingly in one brown streak, there was a little reindeer running madly about the farmyard, pursuing one unfortunate villager who couldn't run as fast as the others.

"That's Vixen," shouted the old Squire, distracted. "Here, catch him quick. He's a young imp. He'll hurt somebody."

Everybody ran about in a frenzy, but Vixen was nimble, and even paused in his mad rush to look impudently over his shoulder at his pursuers. Then he would give a naughty toss of his head as if to say, "Come, catch me," and was off again, leaping over carts and farming implements, knocking a man's hat off with the young horns just beginning to grow, finally clearing a high fence with one bound, and paused

Everybody ran about in a frenzy.

panting on the other side to gaze through the bars mischievously at the hot, breathless group of men.

Nicholas had not joined in the chase; he was standing at the door of the stalls, holding on to his fat stomach and shaking all over with mirth.

"I'll take the lot of them," he cried out. "I don't know what the others are like, but I must have that little Vixen. I haven't laughed so much in years. Why, just to see the neat way he clipped off Ivan Prosof's hat!" He went into another gale of laughter, then made his way through the crowd to the Squire, where he finally concluded the bargain, and acquired not two, but eight reindeer, — Donder and Blitzen, the mamma and papa, with their six children, Dasher and Dancer, Comet and Cupid, and Prancer and Vixen.

To talk about the special meaning of this chapter

turn to page 149

CHAPTER 9
THE NAUGHTY REINDEER

OU'D never recognize the wood-carver's cottage now as the peaceful little dwelling it once had been. In order to shelter his eight reindeer, Nicholas had to build an extra shed which was almost as large as the cottage itself. All would be well if the animals stayed where they belonged, but Vixen seemed to take delight in butting his head against the door of his stall so that Nicholas had to rebuild it three times. He would hear a loud crash and look up from his work with a sigh. "I suppose that's Vixen again. Now if he were only as quiet and gentle as his brothers — well, I don't suppose I'd like him as well," he concluded with a rueful shake of his head.

The little reindeer returned his master's affection, but chose the most noisy means of expressing it. He wanted to be as close to Nicholas as possible and would break down one partition after another, in order that he might finally caper up to the door of his cottage and leap around delightedly until his friend noticed him.

Nicholas tried to be severe. "Now, this time, you'll be punished. I have too much work to do to bother chasing you around." And he would make a mad dash after the young imp, who only treated it as a game and retreated quickly behind a neighboring tree, poking his head drolly around the trunk and almost laughing with glee at Nicholas' fat form panting for breath as he tried to catch him.

Then Nicholas would try coaxing. "There now, be a good little reindeer. If you don't behave, I won't take you out with me on Christmas Eve, and you know we all want to have a fine showing. There's that secret I told you about, in the shed." He finally reached Vixen's side, and placing his arm lovingly around his neck, talked gently and soothingly to the little animal, who looked with soft, delighted eyes at his master.

And Nicholas would lead him back to his stall and return to his work satisfied that once more he had quelled this young rebel. He had no trouble at all with the old deer, Donder and Blitzen; and Prancer, Dasher, Dancer, Cupid, and Comet were gentle creatures who patiently endured all the nips on the ear which was Vixen's way of teasing his more settled brothers.

Nicholas was completing plans for a Christmas Eve grander than any he had ever had. He worked day and night to finish his toy-making; he made a final inspection of the mysterious object in the wood-shed; he scrubbed and curried his reindeer until their hides were sleek and shining. Finally the great night arrived. Nicholas made many trips back and forth to the wood-shed, his arms laden with bright little dolls, houses, boats, and animals. After three hours of preparation, everything seemed to be ready. It was almost midnight. Nicholas opened the stall where his reindeer were waiting and led them out into the yard.

"Donder and Blitzen at the head," he said, "then Dasher and Dancer, because they're the next strongest, and then Comet and Cupid; and then Prancer and — why where's Vixen?"

The other deer looked resignedly at their master and settled down to wait. You might know Vixen would be up to something at such an important time!

Nicholas dashed madly in and out of the stable, calling, "Vixen! Vixen! you young imp, where are you? If I catch you, I'll . . ."

Suddenly there was an answering whimper from somewhere over his head. He looked up; Donder and Blitzen looked up at their bad child; Prancer, Dasher, Dancer, Cupid, and Comet looked up at their mischievous young brother, who was perched on the roof of the cottage, playfully butting the chimney with his horns.

"You bad reindeer! How did you get up there? Oh, I see. Climbed the low shed and then jumped over to the cottage roof. And how are you going to get down, hey? Well, I'll tell you," Nicholas shouted, really angry now, for he would stand no trifling about his Christmas visits to the children. "I'll tell you; you won't get down. You'll stay there, for all I care. I'll leave Prancer at home and take only six. I suppose you are afraid to jump down again, you bold imp! Well, I'll not help you. I'm through with you."

Vixen whimpered again. He was really sorry, and he was really frightened, so frightened that he couldn't remember clearly how it was he had reached the roof. He leaned against the chimney, and wet tears ran down his nose. He looked beseechingly down at Nicholas, but his master turned sternly away and began harnessing the other deer together. Vixen became annoyed. How dare they leave without him! He stamped an angry little hoof on the hard crust of snow. Crack went the crust, and Vixen toppled over on the roof and felt himself carried down the slope, swiftly, swiftly; carried right over the edge, and landed head first in a soft snow-bank right at Nicholas' feet. All you could see of the naughty little fellow were his four hoofs waving madly in the air. Nicholas began to laugh, the other reindeer lifted their heads in the air and seemed to enjoy the scene too, and it was a thoroughly ashamed and meek little reindeer who finally scrambled out of the snow-bank and took his place quietly beside Prancer.

Now for the big show! Nicholas finished tying the eight reindeer to each other with a harness bright with jingling silver bells; he slowly backed them to the wood-shed door, which he opened, disclosing a most beautiful sight. There stood a bright, shining red sleigh, trimmed with silver stripes and stars, the runner curving up in front to form a swan's head, the back roomy enough to hold toys for several villages full of children. Nicholas backed his reindeer into the shafts; he climbed up on the high seat, beautifully padded with cushions made of soft doe-skin; he took out of the socket a long, shiny black whip, snapped it in the air, and they were off!

His four hoofs waving madly in the air.

The villagers were awakened from their sleep by a merry jingling of silver bells, by the stamp of reindeer's hoofs on the hard snow, by the snap of a whip. They peeked out from behind their curtains and saw a brave sight. They saw by the white light of the moon, a shining red sleigh drawn by eight prancing reindeer, whose flying hoofs went as fast as lightning; they saw a well-loved figure perched high up on his seat, snapping a long, black whip in the air with one hand and guiding his reindeer with the other — a big, round man dressed in a red belted tunic, trimmed with white fur, baggy trousers stuffed into high black leggings, and a close-fitting red stocking-cap which flew in the wind. They were not close enough to see how the sharp rush of air made his rosy cheeks even rosier, and nipped his nose so that it, too, was almost the color of his suit, and stung his bright blue eyes so that they twinkled and glistened like the Christmas snow; they were not close enough to see his face, but one and all, as they returned to their warm beds, murmured out of full hearts, " That's Nicholas, on his way to the children. God bless him! "

 **To talk about the special meaning of this chapter**

turn to page 149

{ 83 }

CHAPTER 10
DOWN THE CHIMNEY

NE year, when Nicholas was about fifty years old, and his hair and beard were getting as white as the snow around his cottage, and he was growing as round as the balls he gave the children, a strange family came to live in the village. Not much of a family, to be sure — just one little old man, as brown and wrinkled as a nut, and a thin little girl, who shrank away from the crowd of villagers who had gathered, as they always gathered when something new and strange was happening.

"His name is Carl Dinsler," one woman whispered. "The old Squire's housekeeper told me about him. They say he's very rich. He must be to have money enough to buy the big house on the hill."

"He may be rich," remarked another, "but he certainly doesn't look it. Why, that poor old nag he drove into the village must be almost a hundred, and did you see how poorly and shabbily he was dressed?"

"Yes, and that poor little mite he had with him; she looks as though a good meal wouldn't do her any harm. Who is she, anyway?"

"That's his granddaughter. The child's parents died just a short while ago, away down in the southlands, and they say this old man bought the house up here to be alone."

"He can stay alone, then," sniffed another woman. "Did you see the black looks he turned on us all, when we only came out to welcome them to the village?"

"Yes," sighed another, "but somehow I pity that little one. Who's to take care of her up in that big barn of a place?"

It was lucky the villagers had a chance to get a good look at the newcomers on their first appearance in town; for after that day, little was seen of them. The little girl seemed to have vanished completely; the old man descended the hill only to buy small amounts of food — some fish and some flour. And the very curious ones, who climbed the hill just to see what was going on, came back to the village with strange news indeed!

"Do you know what he has done?" demanded one

small boy of an interested group. "He's nailed up all the gates and left only the front one open, and even that he keeps locked with a bolt as long as this." He spread his hands about a yard apart. His listeners gasped. "Yes, and that's not all. I don't know how you could get into the house, for he's put up boards where the front and side doors used to be and on all the windows. There's not one sign of life in the old place now. You'd never know a soul lived there."

"Why, the man must be crazy," they all said, astounded. "He must be afraid of somebody."

"Afraid, nothing!" one man remarked scornfully. "Unless he's afraid someone will steal his wealth away from him."

"He's a surly old wretch," added the schoolmaster. "I tried to see him the other day to ask if he was going to send the child to school. He wouldn't let me get any farther than the front gate. He wanted to know all about the school, and when I told him the children usually brought vegetables or meat or a few coins each week to pay for their schooling, he snarled at me, and told me to go about my business; that he'd take care of his grandchild's education."

"The poor little thing," exclaimed one motherly-looking

woman, " I'd like to tell that old miser what I think of him."

" Well, this is a piece of news that will interest Nicholas, the wood-carver," said another. " One more child in the village, and a lonely one, too."

" Nicholas knows all about her," they heard a deep voice say, and all turned to see that it was the wood-carver himself, who had joined the group unnoticed. " Her name is Katje. I once knew a little girl named Katje," he went on with a sad, faraway look in his usually merry blue eyes, " and that's why I'd like to do something for this poor child."

" Why, how did you find out her name, Nicholas? "

" She was wandering around in the yard like a forlorn little puppy who's been locked in," Nicholas answered. " I was passing that way and stopped at the gate to talk with her. She says she's not allowed to go outside the fence, and that she can play in the yard only an hour each day. She also told me that her grandfather doesn't want her to mix with the village children for fear she'll talk about the gold he has."

The honest villagers were indignant. " As if we'd touch his old money," they said angrily.

" I don't know what we can do about it," said Nicholas

thoughtfully. "We can't force our way into the house, and after all, it's his own grandchild. I guess we'll just have to wait around and see what happens. I can't believe anyone could stay as hard as that with a little child in the house."

The others shook their heads. "He's hard all through, that old rascal. Why, I'll wager he wouldn't even let her put out her stocking on Christmas Eve."

"That's a safe wager," laughed Nicholas. "He wouldn't open his front door even to let something free come in."

The crowd dispersed, and Nicholas went back to his work-bench; but all through the months that followed, his mind was occupied with the thought of the lonely little Katje. He saw her several times after that, and learned that it was true that she would not be allowed to hang up her stocking. The last time he visited her he had been seen by old Dinsler, who waved his stick at him and told him angrily to keep away from his house and his grandchild. And after that day, Katje was to be seen no more.

Hoping for the best, however, Nicholas carefully made a few little toys for Katje and packed them away with his other gifts, and went on thinking and thinking until, just about a week before Christmas, when he was taking a walk

{ 88 }

around the big boarded-up house, hoping to catch a glimpse of Katje, a wonderful idea struck him. He had been staring up at the forbidding-looking house, all barred and locked, when his attention was caught by the huge stone chimney on the roof. His eyes brightened; he slapped his thigh and chuckled to himself. "I'll try it! I may get stuck, but it's worth the attempt."

Christmas Eve that year was a dark, moonless night. The wind whistled mournfully through the deserted streets, and a cold sleet stung Nicholas' face and covered his sleigh and reindeer with a shining coat of ice.

"Come on now, my good lads," he encouraged his deer. "Trip's almost over; we've only the house on the hill now. It'll probably take me the rest of the night," he muttered to himself, shivering in his red coat and looking like a big snow-man, with the rain and sleet forming icicles on his snowy white beard.

He tied the deer to the front gate and then, taking his sack from the back of the sleigh, climbed from his high seat to the top bar of the fence, and in a moment was down in the yard. He stopped to listen; not a sound could be heard but a few shutters banging in the wind and the sighing of the big pines.

He crept over to the side of the house, where a sort of porch covered one door and made an excellent ladder to the roof. He had a hard time, fat and bulky as he was and encumbered by the sack on his back; but he finally puffed his way up to the top of the porch, and in a few minutes was crouched on the sloping roof of the house.

Now was the dangerous part. The roof was slippery with the sleet and rain that had fallen; he had to take out his little knife and hack away the ice, to form wedges where he could get a foothold. Once he paused breathless, when he thought he heard footsteps in the darkness below. He listened intently, but discovered it was only the impatient stamping of one of his reindeer.

Finally a big shape loomed up above him — it was the chimney. Nicholas stopped to rest a moment, then leaned over the wide edge and looked down into inky blackness.

"Just as I thought," he murmured in a satisfied tone. "The old miser lets his fire go out nights, even such a bitter cold one as this."

He climbed over the edge and then began his slow, perilous descent, feeling carefully with his feet for jutting bricks, pressing one hand flat on the sides, and bracing his

Nicholas paused breathless.

back firmly against the walls, and so slowly made his way through the sooty chimney until he finally felt solid earth beneath his feet.

He stepped out of the fireplace into a room which was only slightly lighter than the black chimney. When his eyes became accustomed to the darkness, he made out the dim outlines of a table and, groping around, found the stub of a candle, which he lit. Then he set to work swiftly. He drew out from his pack a bright blue woolen stocking, which he filled to the brim with little toys and nuts and raisins, for he thought the hungry little girl might like a few sweets. Then he hung the fat stocking right on the fireplace, weighted down with a heavy brass candlestick. He stood back a moment to survey his work and was just leaning over the candle to blow it out and make his difficult way back up the chimney, when he was startled by the sudden opening of a door, and a furious figure dashed into the room.

"Sneaking into my house, eh? After my gold, I suppose! I'll show you how I treat thieves; I'll show you!"

The old man picked up a heavy pair of iron fire-tongs and made a lunge at Nicholas, who rapidly sprang aside, so that the table was between him and the mad old miser.

"Don't be such a fool, man," he said quickly, realizing that the other was in such a rage he was dangerous. "I haven't come here after your gold. Look . . ."

"You haven't, eh? Then what brings you here, if it isn't some thieving purpose? Why do you break into an honest man's house in the dead of night if it isn't for the wealth I'm supposed to have?"

"What brings me here? Look behind you at that stocking there. The other children in the village leave theirs outside their doors, but you have that poor child so frightened she's afraid to ask you for anything. I only wanted to make her feel she was just as good as the others, that she could get gifts the same as they find on Christmas morning."

"Gifts," exclaimed the old man, bewildered, lowering his dangerous-looking weapon. "You *give* things away?" He looked at Nicholas as though he were some strange kind of animal.

"Yes," answered Nicholas, relieved to see the fire-tongs out of sight. "I'll even give you a Christmas gift, you foolish old man. Here, if gold's all you care for, here's more — and more — and more, to add to your hoard!"

And he reached into his deep pockets and poured a

"If gold's all you care for, here's more."

stream of bright gold on the table under old Carl's astonished eyes.

" There, that's just to show you how unimportant *I* think money is compared to the love of a little child, which you might have. Did you ever try to make Katje's eyes twinkle at you? No, you only see the bright glitter of this stuff, and so her eyes are sad, pitiful things when you look into them. Did you ever feel her warm little hand tuck itself into yours? No. Your fingers are satisfied with the cold touch of gold. I pity you, old man, but don't you dare touch that stocking or I'll make you sorry for yourself as well. And now," he finished his tirade and brushed some soot from one eye, " now, will you please show me the way to the door. I don't intend to climb up that chimney. I'll never get this suit clean again! "

He marched out of the room, a ridiculous, stout figure, covered with soot from head to toe, and yet somehow a very impressive person to old Carl, who hastened ahead of him and silently let him out into the black, stormy night.

* * * * * * *

The village buzzed with excitement during the following week. Something had stirred up the old miser on the hill! He had ripped off the boards from his doors and windows;

he had bought a new horse and sleigh; he had stocked his larder with huge quantities of food-stuffs. Next, he interviewed the schoolmaster, and within a few days, Katje and her grandfather were seen on the road leading to the school, the little girl's face beaming up at the old man, her feet skipping along to catch up with his long strides and her warm little hand tucked close in his gnarled old fist.

And all because Nicholas had climbed down a chimney to fill a stocking!

To talk about the special meaning of this chapter

turn to page 150

CHAPTER 11
THE FIRST CHRISTMAS TREE

ERY close to Nicholas' cottage was a thick grove of pine trees, — tall, beautiful dark green trees which lifted their branches high up into the sky and formed a perfect shelter for the ground beneath. Scattered in among the larger trees were clusters of firs, brave little trees, which kept their sturdy branches green all through the cold northern winter and came through each heavy snowstorm with their shiny needles still pointed to the sky.

The children used to love to play in this grove, because no matter how stormy the weather was outside, here they could find a warmer, more sheltered spot away from the bitter winds on the hills and roads. And in the summer time, it was a charming place, with the sharp, keen scent of the pine trees, and the soft murmuring of their branches in the breeze.

Nicholas loved this little grove, for in order to get there, the village children had to pass his cottage, and hardly a group went by his door without one or more of their number dashing in to say " Good-day " to their old friend and to watch him work at his fascinating little toys.

One winter day, toward the end of the year, Nicholas looked out of his cottage window and noticed an entire group of children, all running for dear life away from the grove. At first he thought it was some sort of game, but as they drew nearer, he saw that something must have frightened them. A few of the smaller ones were crying loudly, and the larger boys and girls were dragging them along, not one pausing for breath until they reached the wood-carver's cottage, where they all flocked in and stood still for a minute, panting for breath.

Nicholas picked up one of the babies and tried to soothe him. " Why, what's all this about? All you big boys looking so frightened! Did you see a bogie-man in the woods? "

The larger children began to look a little ashamed of themselves; then all began explaining why they had run so fast.

" We were playing robbers in the pine grove, and it was

Niki's turn to take his side hiding so that they could spring out at us. We were the travelers who were going to be robbed, you see," the speaker explained to Nicholas, who nodded his white head understandingly.

"Well," the boy went on, "I was leading the band of travelers, so I took them back a little way so we wouldn't see where Niki had hidden his robbers. We waited long enough for them to get away, then we started marching back. And just as we reached the spot where we had left the others" — here the boy's voice seemed to tremble a little, and the other children shivered and drew closer to Nicholas — "I saw a clump of evergreens move a little, so I shouted, 'Robbers!' and we all ran over there, and — and . . ."

"And a big black man walked out!" shrieked a little fellow hysterically.

"He wasn't really all black, you know, Nicholas," said Niki. "We heard the other fellows say, 'Robbers!' so we ran out of our hiding place, and we saw him too. He had long black hair and a terrible-looking mustache, and he had gold rings in his ears. And he looked at us and said something we couldn't understand. So we turned around and started to run, and we ran right into a whole lot more

{ 99 }

black men, and there were women and babies with them too."

"Yes, and when they saw us running, they all laughed at us, and said things to us in a strange language," added a little girl. "I wasn't afraid after I saw the babies. Really bad men don't go around with babies, do they, Nicholas?"

"No, I expect not, Sonya. They may have looked bad because they were different from the men you see in the village, but I think I know who they might be. Did they have any horses or carts with them?"

"Yes," answered one boy. "I saw three or four thin-looking horses standing by a big covered wagon."

"I saw the wagon, too," said Niki. "It was big, but one of the wheels had rolled right off, and it looked as though that cart would stay in the snow for a long time."

"You know, I think they might be gypsies," said Nicholas.

"Gypsies!" exclaimed all the children at once. "We never had any in the village before; are they robbers, Nicholas? Will they live here?"

"I don't know, children. Gypsies usually don't wander north in the winter time; this tribe may have lost their way. At any rate, they can't get any farther south now until the spring. Very few travelers can get over the pass in the mountains, and if their horses are old and their wagons broken down, they would be foolish to attempt it."

"But where will they live, Nicholas?" asked gentle little Sonya in a worried tone. "Those poor little babies and their mothers can't stay out in the cold all winter, can they? And there aren't any houses in the village where they can stay."

Nicholas shook his head. "That's true, my dear. But I guess gypsies are used to all sorts of weather. Why, I bet those babies would cry if they woke up at night and saw a roof over their heads instead of the stars."

"I'd like to live out in the open all the time like that," said one of the little boys who had been the most frightened. "Only, how can they hang up their stockings if they have no doors?"

This question drew forth an eager stream of still more questions.

"Yes, Nicholas, you couldn't visit those children, could you?"

"They haven't even a chimney like the old miser's grandchild, but they'd like toys too, wouldn't they? They're like other children, aren't they, Nicholas?"

" Yes, those little gypsies out there in the pine grove are real children just like you, even if their curls are black and yours are yellow." And Nicholas tweaked the locks of the nearest flaxen-haired child, and then Vixen poked his head through the window to see if he was missing anything. So the children forgot the bad scare they had received and started to play robbers with the naughty little reindeer, who was a splendid playmate, because he was always willing to be the one to do the chasing.

It *was* a band of gypsies the children had seen, and just as Nicholas had supposed, they had been caught in an unexpectedly early winter storm which closed all the roads and prevented them from reaching the warmer southlands. A few of the men talked the language of the village and tried to explain their troubles to the sympathetic townsfolk, who generously gave them as much food as they could spare. So the gypsies were not in any danger of starving to death, but there was no chance of anyone having shelter to offer them. They would just have to make the best of their few wagons and tents in the sheltered pine grove, with the thick little evergreens keeping out the bitter blasts of the winter winds.

Once the children of the village had recovered from

their first fright they soon made friends with the little black-haired gypsies, and there were many gay times in the camp. The gypsy fathers would build big fires, then all would gather round, yellow heads shining in the firelight close to gleaming dark heads. And the children would teach each other new words, and the gypsy youths and maidens would dance strange wild dances and sing their sweet haunting songs.

Towards Christmas, the village children entertained their visitors with long stories about Nicholas, — how he came every Christmas on a beautiful sleigh drawn by eight fine reindeer; how he was dressed in a bright red suit trimmed with fine white fur; how he went around from house to house filling stockings with beautiful toys and sweets and nuts; and how he even went down a chimney one Christmas because there was no other way of getting into the house.

The gypsy children were much impressed, and listened with wide-open black eyes at the stories. Then they would look down at their ragged dresses and trousers, or glance over at the rough tents and cluster of fir trees that were their houses, and would shake their heads.

"He couldn't visit us," they said. "We have no doors, and no chimneys, and we never wear stockings."

Little Sonya, who wanted everybody to be happy, reported some of these things to Nicholas, and came away from his cottage with a contented mind, for she knew that the wise smile on his lips meant that he had a plan in his kind old head.

Christmas Eve finally arrived, and this year, after he had finished going to each house in the village, Nicholas, to the astonishment of his reindeer, drove them right past the cottage and out into the forest. He stopped at the edge of the pine grove, where he was met by a dark figure. It was Grinka, the leader of the gypsy band.

Nicholas handed the man some white objects. " Here are the candles, Grinka. Remember what I said you're to do? " The man nodded. " Good! You do your part, and I'll follow along with these things."

" These things " consisted of Nicholas' sack, which he carried along with him as he followed Grinka. The gypsy paused at every little fir tree in the grove, deftly twisting a piece of cord around the base of each candle, and so tying it to a branch. Then Nicholas would finish decorating the tree, tying to the green branches shiny red apples, brown nuts, and of course, a sample of every one of his hand-carved toys. It was a long task, because there were over ten of the little evergreens to be trimmed; but Nicholas insisted on having a tree for every family of gypsy children. So it was almost dawn when they finally finished their work.

"Now for the lights," said Nicholas.

They both went around quickly from tree to tree, touching a taper to each candle, until the whole dark grove was twinkling and glowing like the center of a warm hearth-fire.

"I think that's the prettiest part of it all," said Nicholas, "and you must be sure to awaken the children before the sun gets through the pine trees and spoils the effect."

"All right," said Grinka, "I'll go and wake them up now, before you go."

"Oh, no!" said Nicholas alarmed. "They mustn't see me. The children must *never* see me. It would spoil it all. Now I must go!"

And he jumped into his sleigh and was off, with a jingling of silver bells and a crack of his long black whip.

A few moments after his departure, Grinka had aroused all the children in the camp, and Nicholas should have stayed just to see the joy on the thin little faces as they

"And these are our Christmas Trees."

capered around among the trees, each one discovering something new to exclaim about.

"It's the lights on these lovely little dark green trees that make everything so beautiful," said one child.

"No, it's the gifts!" exclaimed another. "Just look at this pretty little doll I have!"

"It's the fruit and nuts," added one half-starved-looking little waif, who was stuffing his mouth with goodies.

"I think everything is beautiful because it's Christmas," decided one wise little boy.

"Yes, yes, because it's Christmas!" they all shouted, dancing around. "And these are our Christmas Trees!"

 **To talk about the special meaning of this chapter**

turn to page 150

CHAPTER 12
A PRESENT FOR NICHOLAS

OLVIG was one of those timid little girls who hated to go to bed, not just because it was bedtime, but because it was so dark in her little room after the cheery living room of her parents' cottage. She would shriek with fear when a tiny mouse ran across her path, and she would walk miles to avoid going by the village pasture, where terrifyingly big yet gentle cows were grazing. She was a somewhat lonely little girl, too, because certain of the big boys in the village, after discovering how timid she was, used to tease her by making sudden noises behind her back or by jumping at her from dark corners. So most of the time she played by herself or with the smaller children of the neighborhood.

Her father used to grow impatient with his daughter.

"What is to become of her?" he would ask his wife. "Why, she's afraid of almost every living thing and makes up a few extra ghosts and hobgoblins from the other world as well. I'm really worried. Sometimes I think the child must be daft."

"That she's not," returned his wife warmly. "Holly has a good sound little head on her shoulders, and it's only this streak of timidity that makes her seem different from other children. Some day something will happen that will make her forget her fears; I feel sure of it. She's such a good, affectionate child, she'd do anything for someone she loved, even if it took the last ounce of her courage."

"Well, perhaps you're right," answered her husband, "but I hate to see her going on like this. It isn't natural for a child her age to go about alone all the time."

"As long as Holly has her flowers, she'll never be alone," said the mother. "She has such a way with them, our garden is the loveliest in the village, even for the short summer we have."

"Flowers!" exclaimed the big man in disgust. "We have them in the yard in the summer, and then she putters over those flower pots all winter in the house. Silliness, I call it!"

He stamped impatiently out of the cottage and left his wife smiling half-sadly at a little window-box of the "silly" blossoms.

Holly's love for flowers and the luck she had in raising them in the harsh northern climate were really remarkable. As her mother had said, the little yard around the cottage was lovely all through the summer with flowers of every hue. Then, when the first sharp frost of the autumn was felt in the air, Holvig tenderly transplanted into boxes and jars those of the flowers and plants which would keep in the house, and carefully gathered seeds from the others for the spring planting.

Of course, like all the other children of the village, Holvig hung her stocking on the door every Christmas Eve and every Christmas morning discovered the same lovely gifts and sweets. Being an affectionate child, she became passionately devoted to good old Nicholas, an affection second only to her love for her flowers. But, unlike the other children in the village, she couldn't take for granted the open-handed generosity of the wood-carver. She wanted to express in some way her gratitude and appreciation that *someone* did not think her queer and odd because she didn't run about with the other children.

But what could she do? She thought and thought, and finally hit upon something which might please Nicholas. She would give him something that gave her more pleasure than anything else in the world: she would share her flowers with him. She always had enough; in the summer the garden was a riot of color, and in the winter she usually had such a careful way of handling her plants, that there were always some in blossom.

So, thoroughly pleased with her idea, the little girl selected a small bouquet of bright blossoms from her window-boxes, for it was now winter, and bundled herself up in her cloak and cap and started for Nicholas' cottage.

"I'm glad he lives at the edge of the wood," Holvig thought to herself, as she trudged along the road through the deep snow. "I don't think I'd ever get to see him if he lived way in the wood. I never could bear to go that far from the village."

As she approached the wood-carver's cottage, she was wondering what would be the best way of presenting her offering.

"I'd like so much to see him and talk to him," she said to herself. "I'm sure he doesn't know me, for they say he's getting so old now he doesn't remember all the children in the village, but just fills a stocking wherever he sees one. But I think it would be more fun just to leave the flowers outside the door, the way he leaves his gifts. That's what I'll do," she decided, and skipped along until she reached the gateway to the cottage. She stole silently across the yard, and was just about to leave her posies on the doorstep when she was startled by a loud crash from the near-by stable. Her heart almost stopped beating, then raced and pounded with fear as she saw a big animal rushing right towards her. She was too terrified to move; her feet remained rooted in the snow; her icy hands held desperately to the little bouquet of flowers. The awful thing made his way straight to her; she shut her eyes and thought wildly, " I'm going to die. He'll surely kill me." A moment which seemed like a year passed, while she waited silently for death, and then finding herself still alive and not hearing a sound from the wild beast, she slowly opened her eyes and stared straight into a pair of beautiful soft brown ones, which were gazing at her with mild curiosity.

"Oh, it's a reindeer," she said to herself, losing a little of her fear. "It must belong to Nicholas, only it might be dangerous, just the same."

She was still too frightened to move, and finally the reindeer, growing tired of standing still, came nearer and nearer, until his nose touched the little bouquet. He opened his mouth and nibbled a posy. He seemed to like the taste of it, for he started to nibble another. Holvig, too astonished to save the first flower, awoke from her frightened trance when she saw her whole bouquet in danger of being devoured. She flew into a rage. She snatched her flowers away from the deer's mouth and held them behind her back with one hand, while with the other she pushed the surprised head away from her and started to deal sharp rapid blows on his shoulders and back. The reindeer stood his ground for a moment, then turned and fled, followed closely by Holvig, who was still so angry she supposed she could catch the fleet-footed animal.

Suddenly she heard a voice behind her. " Here, here; what are you doing to my Vixen? You're frightening him! "

Holvig turned and saw Nicholas standing in the doorway, fat and rosy, his white hair standing like a halo around his head.

" I frightened him! " gasped Holly. " *I* frightened something? "

" Yes, of course you did," said Nicholas. " Don't you know deer are timid creatures and you shouldn't chase them? "

" But he was eating your bouquet, and I became angry, and — do you really mean to say he was frightened of *me*?

Nicholas laughed a little impatiently. "Yes. My goodness, child, why do you keep saying that? Didn't you think you could frighten an animal like that?"

"No," stated Holvig in a wondering tone. "I never scared anybody in my life. Somebody's always frightening me, you know."

Nicholas looked gravely down into the solemn little face. "Come into my work-room and talk awhile," he said quietly. "I think we shall have to get acquainted."

Then, after they were comfortably installed in the cheery little room and Holvig had been given a bowl of warm milk, Nicholas continued, "What is your name, my dear?"

"Holvig is my real name, but everyone calls me Holly," the little girl answered. "Oh, I almost forgot!" she exclaimed, and she dashed out in the yard again and returned in a few seconds bearing a somewhat bedraggled bunch of flowers.

"They look terrible now," she said sadly. "You see, that Vixen ate some of them, and then I dropped them in the snow when I started to chase him; but I guess there's enough left, if you'd like them. I brought them for you," she finished shyly.

Nicholas was so pleased by this offering, that he wanted to know all about Holly's garden, and her winter plants, and her house, and her parents, and everything. So gradually the story came out, and the kind-hearted old wood-carver soon had a good picture of the kind of life the little girl had led, — timid, always shrinking away from something, never quite happy unless she was alone among her flowers.

"Why, I'd never think you were a timid little girl," he said encouragingly. "I think you did a very brave thing to save my bouquet."

"Oh, do you?" asked Holly eagerly. "I was *really* afraid at first," she confessed truthfully.

"Yes, perhaps you were, Holly. But to do something you think is dangerous when you're *really* afraid is more courageous than if you didn't feel any fear at all. Always remember that, my dear," he said kindly, laying a hand on the yellow curls.

"Yes, Nicholas, I will," promised the child solemnly, " and I'll bring you some more flowers next week."

Then Holly said good-by and left the cottage. As she crossed the yard, she noticed Vixen poking his head at her from behind a tree. Her heart skipped a little, but she shut her lips together firmly, and walked over to the reindeer.

"Boo!" said Holly to Vixen.

And Vixen turned and ran for deer life.

 **To talk about the special meaning of this chapter**

turn to page 151

CHAPTER 13
HOLLY GETS ITS NAME

FTEN after that, Holly brought a bouquet of her flowers to Nicholas, and she and the wood-carver soon became very good friends. Nicholas would sit at his bench and work at his little toys, and Holly would sit on a stool at his feet and talk and talk. Without the little girl's suspecting it, her old friend would lead her to tell him of her fears, and she discovered that talking about them here in this cosy little room made them seem somehow less important.

"Did a mouse ever sit still and look at you?" asked Nicholas.

"Oh, no," said little Holly terrified. "I'd die if he did that."

"Well now, why do you suppose he runs when he sees you? Does he ever run *at* you?" pursued the old man, with a twinkle in his bright blue eyes.

"No, he always runs the other way," said Holly.

"Now I wonder why he does that," remarked Nicholas.

Holly laughed, — a somewhat ashamed little laugh. "I suppose he's afraid of *me*," she said slowly, discovering a new idea.

"Exactly," said wise old Nicholas.

Another time he said in a conversational tone, "Now take rabbits, for instance. Are you afraid of rabbits, Holly?"

"Oh, no," answered the little girl proudly. "That's one thing I know to be even more timid than I am. Why, they'd even run at my shadow!"

"That's true; they are fearful little creatures," said Nicholas. Then he continued, "Did you ever see where rabbits live, Holly?"

"Yes, they go down into little holes in the ground, don't they?"

"Mmmm," answered Nicholas, seeming to be busy examining a little doll's face he was carving. "They must be terribly dark, those little holes, don't you think so, Holly?" The little girl nodded her head. "And yet those little animals you think are so timid go way down there to bed every night and probably don't think anything of it."

Holly's forehead wrinkled. "I see what you mean, Nicholas. But if my room were really as dark as a rabbit's hole, maybe I wouldn't mind; but you see, it's only half dark, and the chairs and tables look so terrible in the dim light that comes through the window. I sometimes think they are goblins."

Nicholas put down his toy and turned a surprised face towards the little girl. "Goblins!" he exclaimed. "Now here am I well past sixty years old, and I never heard of goblins. What are they, Holly?" he asked in an interested tone.

Holly looked confused, then a doubtful expression crept into her voice. "Why, I don't exactly know," she confessed. "But I've always *heard* of them," she ended firmly.

"You little silly," laughed Nicholas tenderly, drawing the child up on his knee. "Now, you listen to me, Holly," he went on seriously. "We're friends, aren't we?"

The little girl smiled lovingly at the kind, rosy face so close to hers and nodded her head vigorously.

"And you believe I wouldn't tell you something that wasn't true, don't you?"

Holly nodded again.

"Well, I'm going to tell you something. There aren't any goblins, and there aren't any bogie-men, and there aren't any terrible creatures who just run around trying to harm little children. If you're a good girl, and say your prayers before you go to bed every night, nothing can harm you. Do you hear me? *Nothing.*"

Holly looked very much impressed.

"It'll be hard at first," she said. "But if I think I see a goblin in my room, I'll just say to him, ' Nicholas says you just aren't, you old goblin!'"

They both laughed, and Nicholas hugged the little girl and told her it was time to run home to her supper.

The winter months passed this way, and when spring arrived, just when it was time for planting, Holly fell sick. All through the short summer weeks, she lay on her bed, weakened by a fever, recognizing no one, not even her beloved Nicholas. He brought flowers to her, hoping that they might bring back the wandering little mind, but she only pushed them away and went on with her delirious ravings of big black giants and horrible goblins. For with her illness, all her almost-forgotten fears had returned, and with a heavy heart, Nicholas realized that all their friendly little talks during the winter had been completely wiped from her mind.

She gradually recovered. The fever left her the same pale timid little girl she had been when she had first brought a bouquet to Nicholas' door. She trembled in her dark little room and, during the day, sat at the window and stared dejectedly out at the bare, cold little yard, where there were no flowers. It was winter again, but this year the interior of her cottage was just as bare of blossoms as the garden, because there had been no flower-growing during her illness.

Holly was more heavy-hearted than she had ever been during her entire life. Everything seemed black to her. Her nights were terror-filled in spite of all Nicholas had told her; but more than anything else she worried because she had no flowers. For long months to come, she would have nothing to bring to Nicholas, — nothing for her kind old friend, who had tried to do so much for her. She pressed her thin little face against the window pane and looked with tear-filled eyes out into her bleak front yard.

Two boys were passing the gate and paused to wave kindly at her. Holly waved back and wiped her eyes. She pushed open the casement a little and called out,

"What's that green stuff you have under your arm, Karl?"

The boys came over to the window. Karl held up an armful of beautiful branches, — lovely little warm red berries scattered among shiny pointed green leaves.

"Why, it's beautiful!" exclaimed Holly, clasping her hands, and her dull eyes beginning to sparkle a little. "What is it? Where did you get it, Karl?"

"We got it in the woods, — way back in the part they call the Black Forest. It grows like this, right in the middle of the winter. I don't know what the name of it is."

"Oh, it's pretty," said Holly again. "But — but — did you say the Black Forest?"

"Yes," answered Karl, "and it's black all right. The sun hardly ever gets through those trees, and if you get lost there, I guess you'd stay lost."

"Yes, sir," added the other boy. "I wouldn't go there alone, I can tell you. Well, come on, Karl. We've got to go."

The two boys went on their way, leaving Holly with the picture of the bright red berries and shiny green leaves still in her mind. How Nicholas would love that cheery little plant! The warm little berries somehow reminded her of him, so bright and rosy. But the Black Forest! She shuddered.

"There must be all kinds of terrible things in that place," she thought. "Wild animals and strange noises, and maybe, behind the trees, — goblins!"

She shook a little; then, suddenly, she had a mental picture of herself in Nicholas' cottage, saying, "I'll just look at him and say, 'Goblin, Nicholas says you just *aren't!*'"

Holly buried her tortured little face in her hands. "Oh, if I only dared to do it," she almost sobbed. "He says to do a thing when you are really afraid is braver than if you felt no fear at all. But that's a horrible place; even the boys are afraid to go there alone. But I haven't any flowers for him! And he's so kind to us children, and spring is so far away!"

So she sat there for a long time, her mind turning from one decision to the other. "I've got to do it, to show him. No, I can't, I can't! Something terrible would happen to me. But he said nothing could harm a good child, and I've tried to be good. It's a bright day; maybe there would be some sun in the forest. If I hurried and found the berries quickly, maybe I could be back again before nightfall. I — think — I'm going to do it!"

And she almost ran for her cloak, before she had a chance to change her mind, and before her mother returned from the village.

Nicholas looked up from his work and saw a little figure flying along the road, right past his cottage and into the woods.

"That looked like Holly," he thought startled. "No, it can't be. She's not well yet, — besides," he shook his head sadly, "the poor little thing would be too terrified to go into the woods. It must be some other village child."

An hour later, however, he was interrupted in his work by a frantic woman. It was Holly's mother. "Oh, I thought she was here," the woman said distracted. "When I came home and found her gone, I was angry that she had gone out while she was still so weak, but I was sure I'd find her with you. Oh, where has she gone? She's lost! And it's beginning to storm!"

Nicholas was rapidly pulling on his bright red coat and fur-trimmed cap. "I'll find her, don't you worry." He looked out at the gray afternoon sky, filled with leaden-colored clouds. Already the air was filled with millions of snowflakes, scurrying and tumbling in every direction, and striking fear in the heart of the man and woman who knew there was a little girl out somewhere in the storm.

"I know where to look," said Nicholas. "I'll take the small sled and Vixen; he's the best one for narrow passing, and he's sure-footed over rocks and steep places. You sit down here and get comfortable, and I'll have your Holly here before the snow covers my front walk."

So the round little figure bustled about, energetic and sound in spite of his sixty-odd years, and in a few moments was lost in the wild flurry of snow.

Holly, meanwhile, had found the red berries with the shiny green leaves, and her joy on seeing the cheerful little plant almost chased away the thoughts of what awful things might be lurking behind the huge tree trunks or hiding on the boughs waiting to spring down at her. She gathered a large armful of the plants, and then started back again, her heart beginning to pound once more as the light inside the forest grew dimmer and dimmer.

"I can't understand it," she murmured, her knees trembling as she tried to find the narrow path. "It can't be any later than three o'clock and the sun was quite bright when I came in here. Oh!" she finished in a terrified tone,

The light inside the forest grew dimmer and dimmer.

as she felt the cold touch of a snowflake on her cheek, then another, then another. " I don't mind the snow so much," she continued as she hurried along in the dim light. " The trees grow so thick I don't think there would be enough snow to block my way, but it's getting darker and darker."

She started to run now, as the snow whirled in white mists around her, wrapping the trees in its ghostly mantle and making little white spirits out of low bushes and shrubs. The wind whistled through the branches and moaned high up in the tree-tops; it caught at Holly's cloak and whirled it around her head. In her terrified fancy, it seemed that some ghostly hand was plucking at her and trying to keep her in this terrible place.

She began to run, her arms clutching her bundle of berries, her head bent to breast the storm, her feet tripping over rocks and stumps hidden in the snow. She breathed heavily; in spite of the biting wind, she felt her head grow hotter and hotter; her heart was pounding so hard she thought it would burst through her ribs.

" I can't see anything," she sobbed. " It's getting darker and darker; I can't lift my feet; the trees are falling on me. OH! " she shrieked aloud as her terrified eyes saw a huge form looming at her through the clouds of snow.

She closed her eyes and fell face down in front of Nicholas and Vixen.

When she next opened her eyes, she was in the wood-carver's cottage. Her mother was holding her in her arms; Nicholas' kind face was bent over her.

" Where are my flowers? " was her first question. " I went in the Black Forest alone to get them for you. Where are they? "

Nicholas put the red berries in her arms. " Here they are, dear. Did you bring them to me? "

" Yes, Nicholas. And I was afraid; but I never will be again. I know that now."

Nicholas wiped his eyes. " You shouldn't have gone so soon after you were sick. But I love the little blossom. What is its name? "

" I don't know, but I liked it because it reminded me of you; it's so round and red and shiny," said the little girl with a mischievous laugh.

" That's funny," answered Nicholas, " it reminded me of you, somewhat. It's so brave and gay growing out there in the darkness and the cold, and the little berries have the blood-red of courage in them. So I think I'll christen your little flower. From now on we'll call it ' Holly.' "

CHAPTER 14
THE LAST STOCKING

EN more years passed, and every Christmas morning the children found their stockings filled with toys and candy and nuts. Poor families found baskets filled with good things to eat, — wild fowl, vegetables, flour, and meal. Sometimes even bundles of clothing for every member of the family were placed on the doorsteps. For Nicholas was now a prosperous old man and shared all he had with the less fortunate townsfolk.

But as the years went on, and his good deeds increased, he was growing more and more feeble. The villagers, who loved and venerated him, grew sad when their children prattled happily on Christmas morning over their toys, and the fearful thought in every parent's heart was, — maybe next Christmas he won't be with us.

One year, a group of men and women called on Nicholas at his cottage with a suggestion.

"We thought, Nicholas," said one man a little hesitantly, "we thought that since it's so cold filling stockings outside the door, and sometimes there are five or six to each family, why couldn't the children leave their stockings inside by the fireplace?"

"Then you could come in and get warm and take your time about it," added one woman kindly.

Nicholas raised his white head from the work he was always doing and smiled all over his rosy face. He placed one gnarled hand, grown old in service for others, on a man's shoulder.

"The idea of you coming here to tell me how to do my work," he joked. "Why, I remember filling an embroidered bag for you when you were tinier than your own children are now. And then they started putting stockings out instead of bags, and now you're going to pull the stockings in. Well, times change, I suppose, and I must keep up with the times. So indoors I will go, and I thank you all for your warm fires."

So after that year, Nicholas would creep into houses on Christmas Eve, and would settle his bulky old form comfortably before the fire and fill the stockings leisurely. The firelight would leap up merrily as if to help him at his work, and the peaceful old face with the halo of white hair and beard would beam warmly at the little toys he stuffed into the stockings, and the wrinkled hands would caress lovingly the little boats and dolls that a child's hands would fondle the next morning.

One Christmas Eve, old Nicholas found it more and more difficult to leave each fireplace for the next house. The warm blaze made him drowsy, and his old bones protested as he heaved himself up wearily to be on with his work. It was slow progress he made from house to house, but he finally reached his last stop, his back tired from the bulky sack, his head drooping with sleepiness, and his heart heavy as he realized how old he must be when the task he had done for so many years was now beginning to wear him out.

The last house was reached, and Nicholas dropped in the settle by the fire with a deep sigh of relief. It was a long time before he recovered sufficiently to start filling the stockings; even then he did it slowly, reaching painfully down to his sack, and each time straightening himself with growing difficulty. He filled four of the five stockings

{ 131 }

The old head drooped drowsily.

that were hanging over the fireplace; then, with the fifth one still empty in his hands, the old head drooped drowsily, and Nicholas was fast asleep.

He awoke with a start an hour later when a man anxiously shook him by the shoulder.

"Are you all right, Nicholas?" asked a worried voice. "I got up to see if the fire had gone out and found you still here, and look, it's almost dawn!"

Nicholas shook himself, then stood up wearily. "Yes, lad, it's Christmas morning, and I haven't finished my work," he said sorrowfully.

"I'll do the last one for you, Nicholas," answered the man kindly. "You just leave the toys and things here and go home to bed. I'll finish it. Go along now, before the children get up and see you."

Nicholas, thinking of his warm comfortable bed, handed the stocking to the man and went out into the gray dawn.

Five minutes later, a little nightgowned boy stood in the doorway of the living room. "Why, Father," he exclaimed in a disappointed tone, "I thought it was Nicholas who gave us the toys, and here you are filling my stocking!"

The child looked ready to cry, but his father, caught

with the half-filled stocking in his hand, hastened to reassure him.

"Your Nicholas is getting old, my boy," he said, "and sometimes he gets so tired we parents have to help him in his work. But don't you forget, it's always Nicholas who leaves you the toys."

"That's all right then!" said the little fellow. "It isn't half so much fun when you think your mother and father prepare the gifts."

"I should say not," said the father sternly, "and you must never doubt Nicholas. Why, he might be so hurt at a little boy thinking he didn't fill the stockings, that he might never come to his house again. Think how terrible that would be!"

"Yes," whispered his son in a frightened voice. "What would Christmas be without Nicholas?"

To talk about the special meaning of this chapter
turn to page 152

{ 134 }

CHAPTER 15
THE PASSING OF NICHOLAS

OLLY was no longer little Holly; she was a lovely slender young girl and led a happy life, her childish terrors long forgotten. She hummed a gay little carol that Christmas morning, as she walked along the road towards Nicholas' cottage, her arms filled with the bright red berries that bore her own name. She still continued the practice of bringing flowers all year round to her old friend, and every Christmas Eve she would go into the Black Forest to gather holly with which to decorate his cottage on Christmas morning.

It was almost noon, and as she approached the house, she noticed how silent and empty it looked without Nicholas' head at the window, bent over his work, and with no smoke coming from the chimney.

"Poor thing," thought the girl affectionately. "He's

probably all tired out from his trip last night. I won't waken him. I'll just go in and make his fire and put the holly around."

She stole silently into the cold little cottage, and soon had a warm blaze crackling on the hearth. She cast an anxious glance now and then towards the closed door that led to Nicholas' bedroom; she was so afraid of disturbing his slumber. But she heard no sound and busied herself decking the walls and windows with gay branches. Then, with one spray still in her hand, she looked around uncertainly, and not finding another bare spot in the living-room, she decided to bring it in to place beside Nicholas, so the branch of holly would be the first thing he'd see when he opened his eyes.

She opened the door quietly and stole over to the bed.

"Why, the darling was so tired he fell asleep with his clothes on," she murmured tenderly.

For the fat round figure lay there, still dressed in the bright red suit with the white fur and the shiny black leggings and close-fitting stocking cap.

"Here's your holly," whispered the girl, bending over Nicholas. Then, with a startled exclamation, she dropped the blood-red blossoms all over the still figure and sprang back, frightened.

"Nicholas, Nicholas!" she screamed. "Oh, he's dead! He's dead!"

She ran bareheaded out into the snow, stumbled blindly down the road into the village, and with tears streaming down her face, called loudly for the townsfolk.

They gathered in little groups to listen to her story. The women murmured in broken tones, between sobs, "He's dead!" and clasped their wondering little children closer, as if to comfort them for the loss of their dearest friend. The men looked down to the ground and up at the sky and every place but into each other's eyes, for no man wanted to see the tears that stood there. "Yes, he's dead," they all sighed deeply. "Who's dead, Mother? Is it Nicholas?" asked the children. "Won't he come to us any more on Christmas Eve?"

And the parents had to turn away from the wide childish eyes because they didn't want to say to them that awful sentence, "Yes, Nicholas is dead."

The bells tolled, and the village was in darkness Christmas night. Vixen and his brothers whimpered in their stalls, and the holly glowed red over a still loving heart in a red suit.

CHAPTER 16
SANTA CLAUS

T was a sad year that followed the Christmas morning of Nicholas' death. All through the long cold winter and brief summer the villagers were reminded of the old friend who had left them every time they saw his closed cottage, with a holly wreath still in the window. They had tenderly put him to rest in the pine grove close to the friendly little evergreens and near the spot where the village children came to play. The eight reindeer were no longer in the stalls behind the cottage; they had been taken back to the big stables on the top of the hill by Katje Dinsler. Many a time in the months that passed, a mother would pick up a little carved doll from the floor and gently wipe the dirt from its face, with a suddenly tear-dimmed eye for the generous heart who had given the toy.

{ 138 }

It gradually entered even the most babyish mind that Nicholas was dead and would come to fill their stockings no more. They cried a little, then the image of the fat, cheerful old man faded from their forgetful childish memories, and so the year passed until it was again Christmas Eve.

"Mother, are we going to hang up our stockings?"

"No, no, child. Have you forgotten that Nicholas is dead and can't come to fill your stockings any more?"

This question was asked and answered sadly in almost every house in the village that Christmas Eve, so different from the other years, when every fire in every hearth glowed warmly on happy, expectant little children who were busy choosing their best and longest stocking to hang over the fireplace. This year, the little boys and girls went despondently to bed, and the night before Christmas was just like any ordinary night, with the parents silently banking the fires and bolting the doors that once had been left open to receive a merry, fat figure in a red suit.

And Nicholas might have been forgotten if it hadn't been for one boy, little lame Stephen, who had a still-warm memory of the kind old man and a childish faith that somehow a big heart like his could never die. So Stephen's parents were astonished when he calmly went about hanging up his stocking, just as he had done every Christmas Eve since he could remember.

"But Stephen," his mother reminded him sadly, "you know Nicholas is dead. You saw him carried from the cottage to the little pine grove; you saw his sleigh and reindeer being taken up to Mistress Katje's house. There's no Nicholas any more, child; don't you understand?"

"But I've *got* to hang up my stocking, Mother; I've got to. I don't believe God would keep him away from the children on Christmas Eve. I believe that he will come back . . ."

"Hush! You mustn't say things like that," exclaimed the mother in a frightened tone. "The dead must rest, my son, and it's not for you to say what God is to do with them. But you may hang up your stocking if you want to," she ended, feeling that even though her son suffered a cruel disappointment, the only way to convince him was to have him find his stocking empty on Christmas morning; then he wouldn't spend the rest of his life thinking that his mother *might* have been wrong.

So that was how, while all the other houses had fireplaces that were growing darker and colder, and the doors were bolted and windows tightly locked, there was one cottage in the village where the latch-string was left out, where the fire still burned warmly on the hearth, and where a lone little stocking was hanging bravely, an emblem of faith in a doubting world.

During the night an old, old woman awoke and moved restlessly in her bed, muttering still half-asleep, " I thought I heard the jingling of silver bells and the tramping of reindeer's hoofs on the snow. No, it must have been a dream," she sighed, and went back to sleep.

Christmas morning dawned bright and clear. It might have been the first Christmas morning of the world, the sun was so warm, the air was so pure and fresh, the snow so virgin-white and glistening as it lay piled up along the fences and doorways. The little village street lay peaceful in the early morning quiet.

Suddenly the tranquillity of the place was broken by a wild shout, the door of one cottage burst open, and the figure of a boy dashed out into the snow, one thin bare leg dragging a little as he limped through the gateway, and one arm waving wildly in the air, — a long, fat, bulging woolen stocking!

" He isn't dead! " shrieked Stephen, his thin face transfigured by a beautiful joy. " Look at my stocking! It's filled, just the same as last Christmas! And there's a big new sled by our fireplace. I knew it! Look, everybody! Wake up, wake up! Nicholas isn't dead!"

Men, women, and children leaped from their beds to see what all the noise was about, and the children leaped right into the largest piles of toys they had ever seen, — all around the fireplaces, on the tables and chairs, and even beside their beds. The entire village opened its doors and poured out into the street, the children dragging handsome new sleds loaded with the most beautiful toys the village had ever seen.

"Did you see this? Look at my boat!"

"He must have come down the chimney when he found the door locked. There was some soot on the floor."

"Isn't it wonderful? It's the happiest Christmas we've ever had!"

"Little Stephen found a fir-tree on his table, decorated with more gifts and fruit and candles, just the way the gypsy children had their gifts, many years ago."

"Yes, and Stephen says there is a big shining star way up on the topmost bough."

"That's because Stephen believed in him," they said,

ashamed of themselves. " But now, *we* believe too. He isn't dead! "

So the bells pealed out on Christmas morning, — a joyful, happy sound, so different from the mournful tolling of a year ago; and the happy villagers almost sang the universal refrain, " He isn't dead! "

The children danced and ran around with their toys; the men looked at each other with solemn, awe-filled eyes; the mothers held their babies close and murmured, " He isn't dead, my pet; you'll grow up and Nicholas will still come to us."

One old woman, she who thought she had heard silvery bells in the midnight air, with her eyes half on another world, said in her cracked old voice, " He's a saint, that's what he is! "

" Yes, he's Saint Nicholas now! " They all took up the shout, and the whole town joined the glad cry, " Saint Nicholas! Saint Nicholas! "

A baby's voice tried to add his stumbling speech to the general shout. " Sant' Clos! Sant' Clos! " he lisped.

" We believe now," the children and the fathers and the mothers all said to each other with the light of faith that little lame Stephen had inspired on their faces. " We believe that Saint Nicholas will always come to us as long as there is one child alive in the village."

"In the village!" echoed little Stephen. "In the whole world!" he shouted triumphantly.

 **To talk about the special meaning of this chapter**

turn to page 152

{ 144 }

The following questions will help readers and listeners better understand some of the "whys" of the Santa Claus legend. They were added to summarize chapters and also to encourage thoughtful discussion of some special Christmas traditions.

Chapter 2, *His First Christmas Gift:* **Why was Christmas a moving day for Nicholas?**

145

Chapter 3, *The Race for a Sled:* **Did the boys wait for Nicholas because they were tired?**

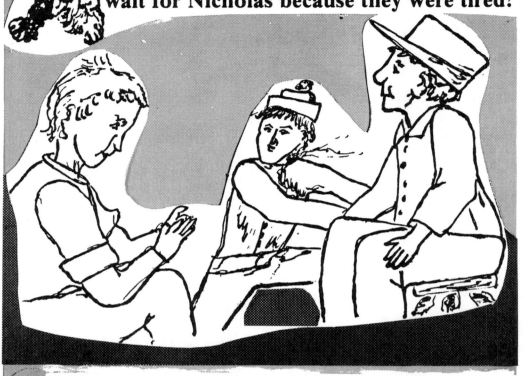

Chapter 4, *Night Before Christmas:* **What made "Mad Marsden" mad?**

Jim Baxter started painting in the 1970s after receiving a watercolor set for Christmas. He is a lifelong resident of Northern New York, who has demonstrated his artistic talent as an expression of his appreciation for the natural beauty of the North Country. An elementary school teacher, he combined his understanding of children with his drawing skill to improve the cover, graphically annotate, and illustrate several parts of this edition of The Life and Adventures of Santa Claus. *Jim lives with his wife, Gail, and their daughters. Deanna and Susan in Potsdam, New York.*

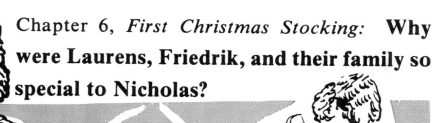

Chapter 6, *First Christmas Stocking:* **Why were Laurens, Friedrik, and their family so special to Nicholas?**

Chapter 7, *Nicholas' First Red Suit:* **Was the red suit really too big?**

Chapter 8, *Donder and Blitzen:* **Why did Nicholas buy eight reindeer?**

Chapter 9, *The Naughty Reindeer:* **What was the big show?**

149

Chapter 10, *Down the Chimney:* **What lesson did the old miser learn?**

Chapter 11, *The First Christmas Tree:* **Why did the gypsy children receive the first Christmas trees?**

Chapter 12, *A Present for Nicholas:* **Who was more scared—Holly or Vixen?**

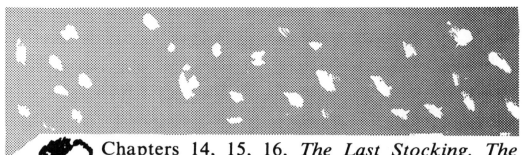

Chapters 14, 15, 16, *The Last Stocking, The Passing of Nicholas, Santa Claus:* **What is Santa Claus?**

To order additional copies of this book send $10.00 plus $2.00 for postage and handling to:
Parkhurst Brook Publishers
Perrin Road RD 3
Potsdam, New York 13676

or
Order from your bookstore:
ISBN0-9615664-18

A teachers' supplement including additional questions and vocabulary builders is also available from the publisher. Call 315-265-9037.

154